Totally Bound Publishing b

Internatio

A Sticky W
Chasing the I

CW01085772

International Men of Sports

AT FIRST TOUCH

T.A. CHASE and DEVON RHODES

AT FIRST TOUCH

Dedication

Thank you to Devon for being a marvellous co-author. It's awesome to find someone whose mind twists and turns like mine.
—T.A. Chase

For T.A., who puts up with my streaky writing habits and surprise secondary characters.
For our very patient editor, Rebecca. You have no idea how much I appreciate you!
And for a very helpful reader who piqued my imagination with the news stories she sent.
Thank you!
—Devon Rhodes

Chapter One

"Hey, King, are you still dating that brunette?"

Ewansiha looked up from where he stood in front of his locker. Padraig O'Leary stared at him, obviously waiting for him to answer his question. Ewansiha had never really understood why Padraig had started calling him King, even though that's what his last name meant. He'd asked O'Leary about it once, and the man had said it was because he was the star of the team and the highest paid, so that made him the king.

"Well, are you?" Padraig stripped off his jersey then tossed it towards the hamper in the middle of the locker room.

"No. She was more interested in being a WAG than having a relationship with me," he answered, referring to the acronym for women in the 'Wives And Girlfriends club'. "Do I look like Beckham? And let me tell you something. She wasn't Posh Spice either."

"Who the fuck cares who she is? Man, the way she looks, she has to be a wildcat in bed." Padraig waggled his eyebrows, and Ewansiha's fellow teammates laughed as their captain held out his hands in the universal sign for big breasts.

Barely able to keep from showing his disgust for Padraig's sexist remarks, Ewansiha shrugged. "She wasn't bad. I've had better."

With that comment, he finished removing his workout gear, throwing it in his locker before grabbing his shower stuff. He was done listening to them since he knew it would devolve into bedroom exploits, and while some of those guys were gorgeous, Ewansiha had no interest in knowing what the men liked in bed.

Being black was hard enough at times because of the racism he'd often encountered over the years. Being black and gay could get him killed. It was wrong and Ewansiha was ashamed for thinking it, but at times he was glad he was bisexual, so he could hide the fact that he liked guys as well behind the women he dated.

Oh, he'd managed to find guys to fuck without worrying about them outing him, but when it came to parties and clubs, he'd bring a woman then he'd lose her for a few hours while he went to find a little male companionship. Most of the time, the women weren't interested in where he went. They were at the events to be seen with famous or infamous people.

Ewansiha turned one of the showers on then waited until the water heated up before he climbed in.

"O'Leary up to his usual bragging?"

He whirled around to see Lukas Schulz standing there, in all his naked glory. Ewansiha took a deep breath, trying not to let his gaze trail over Lukas' chest to his flat stomach and everything that lay beyond it. While he tried to ignore the other men on his team, Lukas was one of the few he couldn't keep from staring at.

"The man is a pig," Lukas commented before stepping into the stall next to Ewansiha's.

"Oh right. Yeah, he is, but he's a stud. Captain of a top professional football team. He has to be a little arrogant." Ewansiha stepped into his shower, letting the hot water pound on his shoulders.

Lukas snorted. "A little arrogance is fine. He's a smug asshole, and it's annoying."

Ewansiha had never heard anyone talk about Padraig like that. Of course, it was how he thought of the captain, but he kept his mouth shut. Ewansiha wasn't the type to rock the boat, and he wasn't interested in getting a reputation as a prima donna. There could only be one on each team and Paolo Lancaster was theirs.

For all of Padraig's bravado and assholishness, he wasn't a prima donna. He was just obnoxious and ignorant. Paolo was their top goalkeeper, and a media darling. All the stupid shit he did was front page news for the tabloids. It was annoying, but Paolo's adventures kept the reporters and paparazzi away from Ewansiha's life, so he didn't make a big deal about him.

"That's true as well. You did well in practice today. How's your knee doing?" Lukas shot him a glance as he ducked his head under the water.

Trying to ignore how good Lukas looked, his hard body glistening with water, Ewansiha grabbed his bottle of shampoo and nodded. "Yeah, it's almost as good as new. A few more practices to strengthen it, and I'll be at a hundred per cent."

Lukas grunted. "Good news, King. Team's not the same without you."

"Ah, but you and Colfer can take up the slack. You're just as good as I am. Why haven't you got the big contract yet?" Ewansiha had wondered that before. Lukas had an insanely fast first touch time—he could get control of the ball and make the ideal move or pass moments later—and he was position versatile. So, when Ewansiha'd suffered his injury last season, he'd been afraid that Lukas would take over his starter's position on the team.

Ewansiha was at the peak of his athletic prowess, but the injury he'd sustained had been severe enough that he knew it had shortened his playing career. His retirement wouldn't happen in the next couple of seasons, but it would happen, and far sooner than he would've liked.

"They're not going to give me more money with you, Padraig and Paolo around." Lukas shrugged. "I'm in no hurry. As long as I don't get injured too badly, I've got time to make it big."

"And the talent too," Ewansiha said as he finished rinsing the soap away then turned the water off.

Scrubbing his towel over his head, he took advantage of the fabric covering his eyes to peer around the edge to get a glimpse of Lukas' tight ass. He'd heard too many athletes being compared to Michelangelo's statue of David, but hell if that comparison didn't fit Lukas to a T. Ewansiha wanted to kneel behind the man and bite one of those firm butt cheeks.

A little cough caught his attention, and he blinked, realising in horror that he'd dropped the towel and was ogling Lukas openly.

"Are you ready for your massage, Ewansiha? We have to ice your knee as well."

After turning, he spotted Sergio, the cute little Spanish sports medicine guy, standing in the shower area. Sergio wore a knowing expression and Ewansiha scowled at him. Yet he was glad that Sergio had come in when he did, or Lukas might have spotted Ewansiha eyeing him like he was his favourite ice cream sundae.

And while there might have been a rumour or two about Lukas whispered in the locker room, there was no proof that he liked guys, and Ewansiha wasn't about to get his ass kicked testing those waters.

"Yeah. The hot water helped, but I need your talented hands on my body, Serge." He winked, knowing Lukas couldn't see him, and Sergio rolled his eyes at Ewansiha's flirting.

Ewansiha followed Sergio into the treatment room where several tables were set up. The sports med guy pointed to one of them.

"Climb up on there while I get my stuff."

He did as Sergio said, looking forward to his massage. Not only because it relaxed his body, and helped his recovery time, but it had been a while since he'd had a man touch him and he was starting to go through withdrawals from the lack of male interaction. By interaction, he meant sex, of course.

It had been a long drought for him, though he'd had more than his fair share of female attention the last couple of months. He wasn't complaining, since he did like sex with women. Just sometimes he wanted to be fucked hard and fast, or he needed someone without having to be gentle with them.

"You have to be careful, Ewansiha," Sergio said softly as he approached the table.

Ewansiha lay on his stomach, propping his chin on his folded arms. He bit back a moan when Sergio ran his hands down his back to get him used to being touched.

"I know, but I wasn't thinking. Lost track of what I was doing." They were in the room alone, so he shot a wicked grin over his shoulder at the Spaniard. "Can you blame me, though?"

His friend glanced over at the half-closed door, then back at him. "No, I can't. Lukas has the second finest ass on the team."

"Who has the first?" Ewansiha puffed up, sure Sergio was going to say he did.

"Padraig O'Leary's ass is a work of art." Sergio sighed. "Do you know I have to think of horrifying things like wrinkly old lady boobs and shit like that while I'm massaging him? If I didn't, I'd be sporting an erection so obvious I'd be poking him in the side every time I bent over the table."

Alarmed at the thought of Sergio drawing the homophobe's attention, Ewansiha sat up, then turned to grab Sergio's wrist and met his gaze. "You have to promise me you will do everything in your power not to let Padraig know you're interested in him… Or hell, try not to let him even think you're gay."

Sergio didn't try to get free. He simply covered Ewansiha's hand with his and smiled. "I might not be as smart as you are, my friend, but I don't have a death wish. I've heard him in the locker room and on the field. I know how he feels about gays. I lust after him in my fantasies, and those aren't going to ever come true because I don't want him to beat the shit out of me."

Releasing both his pent-up breath and Sergio's wrist, Ewansiha lay back down. "I'm sorry, honey. I should've known you wouldn't do anything to endanger yourself, but I'm attached to you. I don't want anything bad to happen to you, and Padraig O'Leary is bad news all around. He's got more talent than any footballer should have, but he's still a caveman in his thought processes."

Sergio patted Ewansiha's ass once before he went to work on the knots in his lower back. "Do you think someone will ever get it through his thick head that he probably knows several gay men, and calls them teammates or friends? And that a gay man doesn't wear the mark of the beast on his forehead for everyone to see?"

Ewansiha huffed in annoyance, then told Sergio a thought he'd had several times after listening to yet another Padraig rant about gays. "I think Padraig is so deep in the closet, he doesn't even know he's gay."

"No way! Do you really think...?" He stopped when footsteps sounded in the hallway outside the room. When they passed by without stopping, he continued, "Do you really think he's gay?"

"There's such a thing as protesting too much, and people who hate something about themselves tend to be very vocal about hating that same thing in others." He had no proof to back up what he was saying about Padraig, just a soul-deep feeling he got every time he listened to the captain spout off his homophobic nonsense. "But don't quote me on that, Serge, and don't take my thoughts to green light doing something stupid like seducing him."

Sergio grinned at him. "What's that saying? Every man's a six-pack away from bisexuality? Though lucky for gay boys everywhere, *you* don't need to be drunk to be willing to have some fun."

Ewansiha reached back to pinch Sergio's ass. "Maybe, but if you keep it up, there's one little gay boy who won't be getting any more of my fun now that I'm free."

Gasping, Sergio straightened then whispered, "The rumour's true then. You kicked that bitch to the kerb."

"I should've listened to you, honey. You had her pegged from the moment you met her." Ewansiha shook his head. "God, if I had to listen to one more comment about when would she get to meet Victoria Beckham, I was going to choke her. Like I hang around with the Beckhams. Hell, they're major celebs. I'm just a footballer, not a brand name."

"I just don't understand the women whose goal is to be a WAG." Ewansiha imagined Sergio shaking his head while saying that. "Doesn't she have any dream that doesn't revolve around a guy?"

"Oh come on. Don't be so harsh. She'll find some guy who's so overwhelmed by her assets that he'll give her what she wants. It's just not going to be me." Ewansiha grunted when Sergio's hands hit a particularly tight spot in his back. "Do you think we can talk about something else?"

Sergio's giggle brought a smile to Ewansiha's face. The guy was a little more flamboyant than he probably should be around the locker room, but he only let out his flaming side around Ewansiha, or at least Ewansiha thought he did. No one else had ever made a comment about the talented young therapist.

"I scheduled your PT session for ten tomorrow morning. You'll need to do an hour of it before you go out for practice, which I already cleared with Coach Kaiser. I'll do another massage, then I'll wrap your knee in ice. The day after tomorrow, you have an appointment with the orthopaedic doctor to check your progress." Sergio started to work on his legs.

"Christ! I need a personal assistant to keep track of all my medical appointments. The only things I remember are the games, and those only because you put them in my phone for me." Ewansiha's eyes threatened to close as his body began to relax from the release of tension.

"Don't fall asleep yet. Roll over and let me wrap your knee with some ice, then you can nap for a little while."

Ewansiha did just as Sergio had suggested, knowing his friend wouldn't let him oversleep or let the ice stay on his knee for too long. Since he'd been given permission to go full out in practice, his knee had been bothering him to the point where he hadn't been getting a full night's sleep, and it was catching up with him.

As he drifted off to sleep, he heard someone say, "Is he all right, honey?"

His last thought as the darkness claimed him was that he'd thought he was the only one who called Sergio 'honey' in the locker room...

Lukas waited in the hallway as Sergio joined him, protectively closing the door behind him and blocking off his view of Ewansiha lying motionless on the table. Lukas knew his concern went beyond that of a player for a fellow teammate, but he didn't want even Serge to know that.

"He's fine, babe. Just exhausted."

"Why would he be so tired?" Lukas asked the question rhetorically rather than actually expecting an answer. He knew better.

Sergio was a fun-loving guy who might seem to the casual observer to be an air-head. But he hadn't got to be a support member of one of the Bundesliga teams by letting his mouth run about his clients. Which was one of the reasons that Lukas considered him to be such a good friend. After all, Sergio had never given any hint of Lukas' biggest secret to anyone else.

A secret that Sergio had intimate knowledge of…

A huff of laughter from Sergio brought him back from his thoughts. "What on earth could you be thinking of right now? The look on your face," the trainer teased.

Lukas met Sergio's amused gaze ruefully. "I can't hide anything from you." They began walking back towards the locker room together.

"Nope. You never could." Sergio stopped in front of his office. "So, will I see you out and about tonight?"

He shrugged. The thought of going out and working off some steam was tempting, but pre-season practices were starting to ramp up…

Sergio lightly punched his arm. "Don't get all 'all work and no play' too soon, Mr Serious. Season hasn't even started yet. Might as well enjoy a few more good nights out before then, hmm?"

His friend was right. Why shouldn't he have a little bit of fun before he had to really buckle down?

"Where are you going to be headed?" he asked. Not that he was angling for a hook-up with Sergio, but hell, if they both struck out in finding someone at least they knew they had some chemistry and a level of trust with one another.

Sergio shrugged, the movement the slightest bit flirtatious. "Probably The Gypsy first, then who knows?" He grinned and leaned in. "I'll have my phone on vibrate if you want to"—he dropped his voice to a whisper—"make me shiver."

The double entendre and breath against his neck gave Lukas a pleasant shiver of his own, and he tipped Sergio a meaningful nod before heading farther down the hall. He was now actually looking forward to a night out, ending with a satisfying encounter with either Serge or someone else.

He refused to let the nebulous image of a random, hot hook-up coalesce into the tall, powerful form of Ewansiha. That was barking up the completely wrong tree, no matter how much he might hope differently. Hell, it would be more likely that that asshole Padraig was gay than it would be King. He'd dated some of the most gorgeous women in the country over the time Lukas had known him.

But damn, he was a beautiful man. Lukas' eyes were always drawn to those plush, soft-looking lips, and King's body was a work of art, and poetry in motion out on the field. He was much taller than Lukas — maybe the tallest guy on the team — but was naturally athletic in a way that made you forget how big he was until you were right up next to him. His absolutely cut musculature was magnified when his dark skin was wet, which was often, between the sweat at practices and games and the showers afterwards. All of which Lukas had to suffer and bite his lip through. He had such a man-crush it was sickening.

Why do I always want the straight guys?

Well, with a body like that, it's such a shame for it to be wasted on women, he answered himself somewhat sarcastically, trying to humour himself out of the familiar disappointment. *He must have to really hold back with the tiny ones.*

That, of course, conjured up an image of Ewansiha *not* holding back, pounding into Lukas, and he breathed in sharply through his nose trying to control his sudden arousal. He wanted nothing more right then than to walk back down the hall, go into the trainers' room and wake Ewansiha up in the most pleasurable of ways.

Get a grip!

Yes, it was definitely time to go out and get with someone who actually wanted what Lukas had to offer.

Chapter Two

Lukas adjusted his sunglasses as he approached the entrance to the club. He wasn't exactly trying to hide his identity, but had learnt early on that if he was recognised, he usually ended up having to leave alone in order to avoid having his hook-ups featured online and in the tabloids the next day. He also had no desire to fend off fans wanting to sleep with him just because he was a well-known footballer. He'd much rather fly under the radar as just another guy, and maybe strike up a connection with someone attracted to his looks rather than his bank account or his fame.

It was always surprising when he looked in the mirror just how much the sunglasses changed his appearance, especially when he was in clubbing clothes rather than sportswear. Without any distinctive tattoos and having a very ordinary short blond haircut, he blended in with the crowd. He had one of the better physiques on display, though by no means the best, and the sunglasses seemed to change his facial features when his eyes were hidden from view.

Just another gay guy on the prowl. He smirked and gave a 'what's-up?' head motion to the bouncer as he walked past and into the interior. He was immediately enveloped in the warm, thumping atmosphere, dark with coloured lights changing to the beat of the music. His shades had been purposely chosen to be light enough to see through, even in the dimness of the club.

Lukas avoided the bar and instead made a circuit of the room, seeing and being seen, keeping one eye out for Serge, though it was a bit early for him. No sign of him yet. He went ahead and ordered a bottle of water from the bartender. When he got it, he paid then took a long drink, leaning back against the end of the bar where he had an overview of most of the room.

He might be looking to have some physical fun tonight, but he was in training, and for him that meant no alcohol. He knew that made him the odd one out—most of his teammates did plenty of celebrating and he didn't think less of them for it. He was completely focused on his lifelong goal of being among the elite footballers in Germany. Everything he did—his schedule, training regime, diet—all was designed towards that end.

Well, almost everything. A guy needed a release sometimes, and being a gay professional footballer didn't exactly fit the mould. Their team captain was one of the most homophobic and bigoted men Lukas had ever encountered, so even though a few of his teammates knew he preferred men, Lukas had never overtly come out, or stood up to Padraig when he went on one of his rants in the locker room. It was hard to hold his tongue at times, but the last thing he needed was a big target on his back. Sponsors would be harder to get and to keep as well, and if he became too 'controversial', his team could decide to not renew his contract. Teammates could also make his life both on and off the field unpleasant in myriad ways, so Lukas took the easy way out and kept his thoughts to himself and his sunglasses on. Hiding in plain sight.

"Hi there." This was accompanied by a not-so-subtle nudge to his side and he glanced over...and down. "Buy you a drink?" A dark-haired beauty was working the angle, looking up at him through his glammed-out lashes. Rather than the sexy vibe Lukas would have expected, though, he seemed brittle — uncertain and maybe even a bit scared.

Lukas barely kept himself from shaking his head — not at the offer, but at just how young the young men were looking these days. He was barely in his mid-twenties and he felt ancient next to this cute little thing. "I appreciate it, but I'm all set." As his admirer's face dropped dramatically and the seemingly genuine look of disappointment tugged at his heart, he felt the need to add, "I'm just not drinking tonight."

That intent gaze flicked from his face to the bottle of water and back. "I can buy you another water." His eyes begged for acceptance in a way that went way beyond a normal pick-up.

Lukas frowned, wondering what was going on with his new friend. His curiosity was going to kill him one of these days. He hoped he wasn't making a huge mistake in opening a dialogue with this one. "Why don't I buy *you* something? I'm Lukas," he introduced himself.

Sheer relief crossed the young man's face and his whole frame seemed to relax at once. It made him look tired. "Xav. Well, Xavier, but I go by Xav. And, um... A drink..."

Lukas took the decision out of his hands by catching the bartender's attention, waggling the water bottle and holding up two fingers. When the drinks had been delivered, he handed a bottle to Xav and scanned the room for a seat. He wanted to talk to the young man and see if he could get him to open up. But the club was filling and about every available space was occupied. So instead he bent down close to Xav's ear.

"Xav, how old are you?"

"Twenty," came the immediate and obviously false answer as Xav drew himself up, as though standing straighter would add years to his appearance.

"Try again. I just want to know the truth, okay?" Lukas persisted and Xav's false bravado wilted a bit.

"Um…"

"Truth," Lukas reminded him.

"Sixteen."

Jesus.

"Sorry to have bothered you." Xav sounded so down that Lukas made a snap decision. Any desire he'd had to find someone to take the edge off with tonight had been extinguished by their encounter.

"Tell you what," he began, choosing his words carefully to make sure the young man had no illusions about what was on offer. "Let me take you out for a bite to eat and you can tell me about yourself. And you can stop with the cute, enticing looks," he added as Xav brightened up at the invitation. "I'm not interested in more than a dinner companion."

"Oh." Xav's gaze flicked around the room before he sighed. He looked back at Lukas soberly. "I'd like to, but… I really need to go home with someone tonight."

Something in the way he'd worded that started things ticking over in Lukas' head. "You actually want sex? Or you need a place to stay?" he asked as gently as he could.

He knew he'd hit the nail on the head when Xav's lower lip trembled before he pressed his lips together tightly. "A place to stay," he admitted quietly, his eyes huge in his face. "But most of the time you have to do the first to get the second."

Lukas' insides twisted in a gut-roiling combination of sympathy and anger. He thanked whatever deity existed that Xav had come up to him tonight instead of some other, less moral guy. He tried not to think of previous nights and what Xav might have gone through.

"Not with me," he said firmly. "Come on. Let's get out of here." Xav didn't move right away, and Lukas tried to reassure him. "No pressure. Just dinner and a place to crash tonight if you need it. Okay? Seriously—no offence, but I have zero interest in a kid your age."

Conflicting expressions of curiosity, wariness and hope flickered across Xav's face in rapid succession. "Why are you being so nice? You don't even know me."

Lukas wasn't even sure himself. He began walking, cupping Xav's elbow to usher him along and to his relief, he gave no resistance. "You seem like a good kid who's had to grow up too fast." He shrugged. "I had it easy. Maybe I just want to help."

There was no response and he looked down at Xav walking willingly by his side. He dropped his grip from his elbow as they approached the exit then was startled when Xav moved closer and slid his hand into the crook of his arm, as though Lukas was escorting him. He pressed even closer as they neared the bouncer, and Lukas got the impression that he was nervous about the man. He deftly moved Xav across in front of him until he was walking on the opposite side as they passed.

Another question to add to the list of what he needed to know from Xav.

But first, dinner.

Just as they were almost out of the door, Lukas spotted Sergio coming in, dressed in clubbing clothes very different from what he wore to work. 'Dressed' might be stretching the description a bit. His pants— either leather or some facsimile—looked painted on, and Lukas had a feeling that his unbuttoned shirt would be coming off in about five seconds. He spotted Lukas and made a beeline for him.

"Lukas! You did come. I'm sooo glad." He swooped in for a brief kiss and grope of his ass. Then he did an almost comical double-take as he finally realised Lukas had company. Sergio frowned at Xav before shooting Lukas a questioning 'What the hell?' look.

He beckoned Serge to follow them back out of the door, keeping an eye on Xav's reaction. He was eyeing Sergio warily but didn't budge from Lukas' side.

"Um… He's a bit…young for you, isn't—?"

"Yes, which is why we're just going to grab a bite to eat," Lukas interrupted Sergio's incredulous statement of fact. At Serge's sceptical expression, he added, "You're welcome to join us if you like."

Sergio narrowed his eyes shrewdly, studying Xav. Lukas felt him grip his arm even tighter. He pointedly raised his eyebrow at his friend, who finally nodded. "Sure. I was planning on drinking my dinner, but I know calories from food would probably make you happier with me."

Xav looked like he had no idea what to do now, and Lukas could sense that he was about a second away from calling the whole thing quits and disappearing on him.

"Come on, let's go then. I have a feeling this one's really hungry. Still growing. You remember those days, don't you?"

Sergio's expression softened a tad. "Like they were yesterday. Which they were. I'm not *that* much older than you. Okay. Just across and down a block is a good café that's open late. We can probably still get a table if we hustle."

He turned word to deed by leading the way at his customary fast clip along the sidewalk to the corner, then crossed the street. Lukas and Xav trailed along in his wake as he wove easily in and out of late night revellers in the nightclub-laden part of town.

Sergio breezed into the café's entrance and was already being led to a table by the time they'd caught up with him.

"Thank you, beautiful," he said to the hostess who'd seated them, adding a wink for good measure. Her gaze dropped to his nearly bare chest as she turned away and he grinned wider before buttoning up. To Lukas' knowledge, Sergio had zero interest in females—he was just a consummate flirt and no one was safe from being on the receiving end of his wiles. Except, hopefully, Padraig.

"Do you know what you want to eat, Xav?" Lukas asked. The young man hadn't said a word since before they'd left the club and he was beginning to become concerned.

Xav parted his lips as though to answer, then shrugged, toying with his menu but not really looking at it.

Lukas began to regret inviting Sergio to join them. Xav seemed incredibly uncomfortable in his presence and the barriers had gone way up. Sergio continued to watch Xav closely, and Xav squirmed under his regard. He glared at Serge, wishing he'd cut out the examination.

Xav finally tossed his menu aside. "I don't want to get in the middle of you two. I mean, I don't want to cause trouble. I'd better go." He pushed back in his chair and made to rise, but Lukas stopped him with a gentle but firm grip on his arm.

"Stay. I promised you a meal at least. Serge, be nice."

"I *am*," Sergio protested. "Just wondering what the story is here. Seriously, you do *not* need the kind of publicity getting photographed alone with this boy would give you. Which is why I came with you as a chaperone. You're welcome."

"Photographed?" Xav asked with a confused expression. "Are you someone famous or something?"

"Or something," Lukas muttered before answering Sergio. "I doubt anyone recognised me anyway."

"You'd better hope not, especially not with club-baby on the make here." Serge cocked his head and looked at Xav. "You're not a pro, are you?"

Xav furrowed his brow, then his eyes widened dramatically and he shook his head.

The server arrived, so they decided on their meals, with Lukas ordering more than he needed in case Xav's appetite really exceeded his modest request. Once they were alone again, Lukas turned to Xav.

"What exactly did you mean about getting between us?"

Xav shifted in his seat. "Well… Aren't you like a couple or something? I mean, you fight like one and he kissed you, so I thought…" He trailed off as Sergio and Lukas both laughed.

Sergio leaned in and patted Xav's hand. "First of all, no. We're just friends. Well…for the most part. And since I don't think that Lukas will be doing anything with you that would affect a relationship anyway, it wouldn't have really mattered."

Xav's relief was evident in his expression and he relaxed again.

Lukas felt a pang of empathy at how close to the surface all of Xav's emotions seemed to be. He hadn't yet developed a hard skin, which might be a good thing. Maybe things hadn't been as bad as Lukas had feared. "Thank you for being concerned, but there's nothing to worry about. We're all friends here. So why don't you tell us a little bit about you?" Lukas encouraged.

The young man paled a bit and avoided eye contact. Lukas could almost see him trying and discarding different answers.

"Truth," Lukas repeated his warning from earlier in the evening, and to his gratification, it seemed to have the same effect as it had then.

"I'm just…on my own now. My parents… They didn't want a gay son, so when they found out a couple weeks ago…" He paused and let that thought go unfinished. "I thought I'd be able to get a job, find a place to live, but it's hard when you don't already *have* a place. So, well, I go to the club each night and, you know…" He shrugged, looking down at his hands on the table miserably. "I picked you tonight because you seemed nice."

Lukas met Sergio's horrified gaze. He swallowed past the lump in his throat, wishing that Xav had had parents like his own, who, while they hadn't been thrilled to learn of their athletic son's 'unusual' bent, had at least continued to claim him as their own and supported him in their own slightly bewildered way. That involved a great deal of avoidance of the topic, which was just fine with Lukas.

Their food arrived, and Xav didn't waste any time in tearing into his. Lukas' meal was bitter on his tongue, considering everything, and he ended up giving half of his plate to Xav. He noticed that Serge, who had ordered the same thing as Xav, had surreptitiously given him part of his meal as well.

It wasn't until Xav had started to slow down that Lukas returned to their conversation. "Where have you been sleeping?" he asked, and got an arched eyebrow in response. He winced as he realised that was evident from his story, at least the club pick-up part of it. "Every night?" he tried to clarify.

"Well, no. If I strike out or get asked to leave before morning"—his voice was nearly a mumble at this point—"I bench-surf in the park."

"Jesus, kid. You could get killed!" Sergio burst out, looking extremely upset. "Can't you go to a shelter, or—"

Xav was shaking his head. "It's sometimes worse in there, from what I hear. Especially since I don't have anyone to watch my back. Plus, they give priority to families." He sighed. "And I'm a minor…" He took a sip of water.

Lukas had heard enough. "Xav, I want you to come stay at my place." Sergio turned his way, but Lukas didn't look at him, instead watching Xav intently. "I want to help you get on your feet and give you a safe place to live."

Xav, completely still, stared at him for a long time then switched his gaze to Sergio. He dropped his eyes then raised them to meet Lukas'. "Do you want—?"

"I think I've clarified that I don't want a damn thing from you, and I especially don't want you offering ever again," Lukas growled then eased up when he noticed Xav's unease. "I just want to help you out. Pure and simple."

"I don't know. I mean, he thinks you might get in trouble…" Xav nodded towards Sergio.

Sergio interjected, "Oh hell, kid, take his offer. If it comes right down to it, I'll vouch for the fact that there was nothing but altruistic intentions." He waved the server down for the bill. "So where do you stash your stuff?" He impatiently threw down some bills and rose.

Lukas hadn't even thought of that, but Sergio was right. Xav must have more than the clothes on his back. He stood to join Sergio and Xav followed suit.

The beginnings of a smile hovered at the corners of Xav's lips. "Inside a tree," he confessed.

Lukas laughed, relieved to see the stress on the young man's countenance easing the longer he spent in their company. "Well, let's go retrieve it. This I've got to see. Then we'll head to my house. All right?"

Xav looked at him with something like gratitude before he averted his gaze, his eyes suspiciously shiny.

Sergio didn't look unaffected either. He roughly cleared his throat. "Yes, well, I think I'll call it a night after all. Too full to dance. Lukas, I'll see you tomorrow at the stadium, okay? Let me know if you need anything," he finished with a meaningful emphasis on the last word and a quick cut of his eyes to Xav.

Lukas nodded. "Thanks, man. I think we'll be just fine." He gave Xav a quick side-arm hug then released him to give Sergio an embrace.

"Thank you," Lukas whispered quickly.

"Just be careful," Serge returned just as quietly then stepped away and left with one last wave of his hand.

Lukas smiled at Xav and got an actual smile in return. "Okay, let's go grab your things and then head home."

Chapter Three

"Hey, King, I need your ex's number," Padraig told Ewansiha as they strolled into the stadium for practice the next day.

Ewansiha shot him a glance. "Are you sure? She's a vampire, man. She'll suck your soul from you, and leave you wondering what bus hit you."

"Sounds like my kind of woman." Padraig bumped their shoulders together and leered.

"I'll give it to you after practice. I think you two belong together." Actually he didn't think that. He wasn't sure who he'd feel worse for—Padraig or his ex—since he was pretty sure Padraig was gay, but deep in the closet. But his ex-girlfriend was a harpy and he really wouldn't wish her on his worst enemy. He couldn't say that to Padraig, though. They didn't have that kind of relationship.

"Thanks. Of course, I'm only looking for sex right now. You know, so many women to fuck and not enough time in the day." Padraig nodded towards the small crowd of women standing near the entrance of the stadium.

Ewansiha shook his head. "If you put all that energy you spend trying to sleep with women into your football skills, you'd be one of the highest paid players in the league. You have talent, Padraig, you just allow yourself to be distracted by other things."

"Man, you're too serious. Maybe you need to find a new girl to warm your bed. Get that stick out of your ass." Padraig scowled at him before moving off to flirt with the groupies.

"Fuck you, asshole," Ewansiha swore under his breath. Then he winced as he thought about his mother, and how she'd always told him that intelligent people didn't use swear words. It wasn't that he thought he was smarter than the men he played with, but he loved his mother, so he tried to live up to her expectations.

After pushing open the locker room door, he wandered over to his locker, then set his duffle down in front of it. He dropped to the bench as his knee twinged. *Probably shouldn't have gone on that run last night.*

He'd been feeling irritated and frustrated, so he'd decided that getting out of his house might help. He should've known that his knee wasn't quite up to that amount of punishment, especially since he'd had an all-day practice earlier.

Hearing a commotion, Ewansiha looked up to see Sergio and Lukas walk past, heads close together like they were sharing secrets. He didn't fight the urge to stare at Lukas' ass, which was nicely covered by a pair of faded jeans. He shifted on the bench as his cock stiffened at the sight of Lukas. Frowning, he dropped his gaze to the floor. Padraig was right. He really did need to get laid, but instead of holding a soft and curvy body in his arms, Ewansiha wanted a hard and angular one sharing his bed.

Maybe he should go out to the clubs tonight and see if he could find someone willing to come home with him. He'd picked up men before without being outed, though it was difficult. Sergio's laugh drifted from the sports medicine rooms, and Ewansiha considered asking him out for the night. They would both know what would happen after dinner, but he thought about how much he liked the younger man, and he couldn't bring himself to use him just to make himself feel better.

He'd slept with Sergio before, but he knew Sergio wasn't the man Ewansiha would spend the rest of his life with. His phone rang before he could get depressed about being alone at his age.

After digging it out of his pocket, he checked the screen, then answered. "Hello, baby. What's going on with you?"

"Hello, Ewansiha. I'm going to be in town tonight, and wondered if you wanted to get together for dinner." Silvia's voice was smooth like the most expensive whisky.

He grinned at the thought of being able to see his favourite girl. Silvia had been one of his first girlfriends, and she was the one who'd helped him come to the realisation that he liked men as much as he did women. In fact, she'd been part of his first gay experience. She'd convinced him to have a threesome with her and one of her gay friends.

Silvia trusted the man, so Ewansiha had gone along with it, and had ended up dating the guy for a month or so after Silvia had broken up with him. She was his best friend, and the one person besides his mother who would call him on his bullshit if she thought he needed it.

"I'd love to get together with you, Sil. What are you doing in town, though? I thought you had a month-long photo shoot in the Caribbean." Ewansiha chuckled. "I can't believe you got homesick for Germany after being in the Islands."

Her laughter warmed him. "I had to come home for a few days to do some interviews. I fly back out in a couple of days to rejoin the shoot."

"A woman's work is never done, honey." He leant back against the partition of his locker. "Where would you like to go tonight?"

"I've already got us reservations at Lorenz Adlon for eight. I'll expect you to pick me up at seven forty-five at The Regent." She'd always been in charge of their dates when they were together. Ewansiha had just gone along with her.

"Where's Wendy? I'd thought she'd meet you when you were in town."

The room began to fill as the rest of the team arrived for practice. He turned his back on them, not wanting them to overhear his conversation.

Silvia sighed. "She's on a different shoot in Russia, and couldn't get the time off. But she's coming down to Bermuda in a couple of weeks so we can hang out."

"Sorry to hear that, honey. I know you probably miss her like crazy."

Silvia had met Wendy a couple of years after she'd broken up with Ewansiha, and they'd fallen in love. It was her own bisexuality that had helped Silvia detect Ewansiha's tendencies. He'd met Wendy and discovered why Silvia had given her heart to the woman.

"Next time the two of you are in the city together, call me. I'd love to be seen with two beautiful women." He smiled as her laughter echoed over the phone.

"We'll do that, but you do know neither one of us will be sleeping with you, right?"

"I'm not looking for what you've got, Silvia. Not at the moment anyway."

The coach entered, and Ewansiha knew he had to end the call then get changed into his kit.

"I've got to go, Sil. I'll be there to pick you up tonight. Love you."

"Love you too, Ewansiha. We'll talk more tonight." She hung up, and her last statement before she did so made him wonder if maybe he shouldn't go out with her. It sounded like she had something on her mind, and Silvia could be difficult when she wanted something.

He shut his phone off then set it in his locker. His mind kept running through things Silvia could possibly want to talk to him about, but he couldn't think of anything. Ewansiha changed while his thoughts were elsewhere.

It wasn't until he was tying his boots that he realised someone was sitting next to him. Glancing over, he was surprised to see Lukas next to him. Their lockers were across the room from each other. Why would he be sitting there?

"Can I help you with something?" Lukas met his gaze, and Ewansiha saw exhaustion in his eyes. What had the man been doing the night before? "You look whipped, man. How late did you stay out?" Ewansiha shot a glance over to where the coach stood chatting with Padraig. "You're an adult, and you know what you should be doing, but you need to be careful about going out and partying all night."

Lukas blinked at him, like he was surprised Ewansiha would say anything. After making sure there wasn't anyone near them, Ewansiha reached out to rest his hand on Lukas' knee. The flex of muscle under his hand distracted Ewansiha for a moment. He tightened his grip, then stroked his fingers over Lukas' hairy thigh.

"Umm…" Lukas cleared his throat and Ewansiha jerked his hand away.

What the hell are you thinking? He wanted to slap himself in the forehead. He'd always thought Lukas was gorgeous, and he would love to get the man into bed, but he'd never made a move on him because he'd never thought the man was gay.

"Sorry. Got thinking about something else," he muttered.

Lukas shook his head. "No problem, King. Just so you know, I wasn't out partying last night. I'm not Paolo or Padraig. I might go out to the clubs during training and the season, but I wouldn't do it if there was a chance it would ruin my chance of playing. I was helping a friend last night, and ended staying up later than I planned."

"Oh, that's good, because no matter how talented those two are, their late nights and too much drinking are doing them more damage than good." Ewansiha gestured to where Paolo leaned against the wall, head in hand, very obviously nursing a hangover. "If you want my position on the team, you have to work to earn it."

"I know, and trust me, I plan on taking your spot before too long, but I do know you've got some good years left in you." Lukas winked. "The reason I came over here is to see if you'd like to do some drills with me during the special skills practices."

Ewansiha nodded. "Sure. I can show you some of the little things I do to get more power on my kicks."

"Great." Lukas stood, and Ewansiha quickly shifted his gaze from Lukas' groin, not wanting to look like he was staring. "Thanks, King."

Grunting, Ewansiha finished tying his boots, then grabbed a towel from the pile by the door as he walked by. It was time to get to work.

* * * *

"Wendy and I want children," Silvia announced once they had placed their orders and were alone at their table. Or as alone as a well-known footballer and one of the world's top fashion models could be.

There had been camera phones trained on them from the moment they had stepped from his car, but they had both learnt how to ignore them, and to give themselves the semblance of privacy.

As shocked as he was by Silvia's pronouncement, Ewansiha kept the expression from his face. It wasn't that he didn't think either woman would be a great mother. It was simply that he thought they would want to wait longer for them. Both Wendy and Silvia were at the top of their profession, and children were a full-time job in and of themselves.

"I'm a little surprised," he admitted before taking a sip of water.

Silvia gave him a narrow-eyed stare. "Why? Don't you think Wendy and I would be good parents? Do you think we're too shallow or wouldn't want to ruin our figures with pregnancy?"

Ewansiha held up his hand, stopping her in mid-verbal attack. "Wait a minute, Silvia. Have I ever said anything about you two being shallow? Without it being a joke? Do you seriously think I would think something like that about you? You know me better than that."

Sighing, she nodded as she covered the hand he'd left on the table with hers. "I know that, and I'm sorry. It's just our parents have been giving us a really hard time about the whole thing, and I just want someone to support us, damn it."

"Honey, I'll support you through the whole thing. I think you ladies will be wonderful mothers." He brought her hand up to his mouth, then kissed her knuckles. "And I'll get to play the uncle who spoils the kid rotten."

"Well, we were hoping you'd get to be more than the child's uncle." She dropped her gaze, and the hesitant tone of her voice made him suspicious.

"I don't have a problem being a godparent either, though you know I'm not very religious." He grinned at the thought of spending time with a kid and being the one to teach him how to play football. Ewansiha had never really considered whether he wanted kids or not. His two brothers had three kids each, giving his parents plenty of grandchildren.

Silvia shook her head. "No, Ewansiha. We want you to be the father of our children."

The sip of water he'd just taken almost came spitting back out when he heard what she'd said. "You want me to be *what*?"

Their waiter arrived at that time with their meal, though Ewansiha wasn't sure he'd be able to eat after Silvia's statement. She waited until they were alone again before she continued.

"Wendy and I talked about it when we decided to start our family. We want you to be the father because you are the best man we've ever known." Tears filled her eyes. "We thought about adopting, but we decided to try to get pregnant first."

"And since neither one of you is male, you have to bring one in," he mumbled, shoving the food around his plate.

"Right." She reached out to touch him, but stopped right before her hand landed on his arm. "I know it's a shock and everything, but it's not like we're asking you to have sex with either of us."

"No?" He tried to hide his relief, but couldn't quite manage it. He might have slept with Silvia while they were dating, but once they'd split up, he'd never made a move on her. At this point in their friendship, he didn't want to sleep with her anymore. Wendy wasn't bi, so she had no attraction to Ewansiha at all, which in turn did nothing for him.

She chuckled. "Try to sound a little disappointed, Ewansiha. You're hurting my ego by how reluctant you seem to actually sleep with me again."

He chuckled while his head whirled with what she'd said to him. "It's not that I wouldn't sleep with you again, Sil, but I wouldn't do it knowing you're in love with Wendy. No matter if Wendy agreed to it or not. I don't poach on other people's property."

She understood what he meant. "I guess it's a good thing that we just need your sperm. If you agree, we'd make an appointment with a fertility doctor, and he would do the procedure. There would be no touching of intimate parts between us."

"So I'd have to jerk off into a cup or something, and they use my guys to do the deed? One of you would be having my baby?" His hand trembled, and Ewansiha put his fork down before he dropped it.

He met Silvia's soft, dark gaze, and she smiled at him. "I'll be carrying this one if it works. We drew straws and I won."

"This one? Are you planning on having more than one?" He hadn't been able to wrap his mind around the fact that she wanted to have one baby. The possibility of more was short-circuiting his brain.

"I'll tell you what our plans are, but you don't have to decide right away, Ewansiha. We both understand that this is a big decision for you as well. You'll be the baby's father, but you won't be responsible for the raising of him. Wendy and I have more than enough money to take care of ourselves."

"I'm just going to be the donor—hand you a cup of my sperm, then walk away without a care in the world?" He wasn't sure he liked the idea of that.

She shook her head sharply. "No, that's not it. You would be the children's father, and we would acknowledge you as such. We would draw up papers stating visitations and things like that. Whatever you want, but he would be ours. Mine and Wendy's. How about you would have no financial obligations to him? It's not like you knocked one of us up accidentally or anything like that."

Inhaling, Ewansiha realised he needed to hear everything Silvia had to say before he could even begin to make a decision. But he had to admit, he wasn't leaning towards saying no. Silvia had been his best friend for over a decade, and the one person who'd helped him accept who he truly was. If she wanted this more than anything in the world, he would more than likely end up giving it to her.

"Tell me what your plans are, then I'll think about it. I'm not saying no, but I'm also not saying yes just yet, Silvia. I truly need to work it straight in my mind."

She nodded once more, then gestured to his plate. "We can eat while we talk. It's good food, we shouldn't let it go to waste."

"You're right."

They settled back to finish their meal while Silvia explained what plans she and Wendy had made to bring a child into the world.

Chapter Four

What the hell had Silvia been thinking? Ewansiha jerked the laces on his running shoes so tight he almost broke them. He didn't know if he should be honoured or freaked out by what she'd asked him.

After straightening, he began his stretches, which were so automatic for him by now that he didn't need to think about them. He kept going over her request in his head, trying to get a grip on it.

He started jogging down his driveway to the street. Turning left onto the sidewalk, he kept a steady pace. Running at night wasn't the best idea, and he knew that, but he couldn't stay inside his house anymore. He needed to move, and he always seemed to do his best thinking while he ran.

The rhythm of his feet hitting the pavement soothed him, and he let the shock settle through his body. He wished he had someone to talk to about the whole situation, but he'd never really made friends easily. While he had a few friends, none of them were ones he felt comfortable calling at midnight to talk.

Maybe he should call his mother. She wouldn't be shy about how she felt about the ladies' request, but he also knew she didn't have a very good opinion of Silvia. In fact, he was pretty sure his mother blamed Silvia for Ewansiha's bisexuality. Like she'd tricked him into liking guys as well as girls.

Snorting softly, he shook his head. No matter how many times he tried to explain that liking both sexes was something he had been born doing, and there was no way to make someone bi—or gay, for that matter—his mother chose to ignore him.

Of course, since she'd only seen him dating women, she believed his gay half was simply a phase, and to help her with that illusion, he'd never brought one of his boyfriends home to meet her. Amazingly, Ewansiha's father had no problem with his bisexuality.

When Ewansiha had told him, his father had just shrugged and told him that one of his great-grandfathers had been gay, so the genes must have combined in the womb. He'd had a good laugh with that one.

He paused to catch his breath, then glanced around. He'd run a good ways, and he recognised the house he stood in front of. It was Lukas'. Staring up at the front of the house, he wondered if Lukas was home or if he had gone out again.

Ewansiha remembered those days when he had been young and an up-and-coming footballer. He would go out every night, hang out with other teammates and have fun. Then one day he'd realised how much damage he was doing to himself with those late nights and alcohol. So he'd made a change, and had chosen to focus on his career instead of his social life. Not to say that he still didn't go out once in a while, but he did it during the off-season.

After spotting a light on in one of the windows, Ewansiha headed up the driveway, not really thinking about what he was doing. All he suddenly knew was that he wanted to talk to Lukas, even if it wouldn't be about what was really on his mind. Silvia and Wendy hadn't gone public with their relationship yet, and Ewansiha would never do anything to 'out' them, not even to another friend.

As he climbed the front steps of Lukas' house, he wondered if Lukas was a friend. They'd been teammates for a couple of years, and Ewansiha had always been attracted to him. Yet being unwilling to act on that attraction might have made him come off as a bit of an ass at times to Lukas.

After pushing the doorbell, he paced around the porch, keeping his muscles warm and relaxed. When no one came to the door after a little while, he considered that Lukas might not be home, and was just one of those people who left a light on so they didn't come back to a dark house.

I'll give it another ring, then if no one comes, I'll go back. He hit the doorbell again. This time he stayed near the door and shortly he heard footsteps coming towards him from inside the house.

He began talking the minute the door started to open. "I'm sorry, Lukas. I didn't mean to wake you. I forgot how late it was, but I was out running…"

Ewansiha's voice trailed off when he met the sleepy eyes of a young, dark-haired man. The kid leaned against the doorjamb and yawned. Ewansiha's gaze trailed down his naked chest to where his too-big sweats barely hung on the points of his hips.

"Umm... I'm sorry to wake you. I was looking for Lukas." He was a little at a loss for words at the beauty of the man, yet Ewansiha knew he was way too young for him. In fact he would've thought he was too young for Lukas, but hell, he really didn't know the man.

"Lukas is in bed, sleeping. I can go get him for you if you want." The kid shoved a hand through his longish black hair, and the movement drew Ewansiha's attention to the bruises covering his arms and chest.

Who the hell is beating this kid up? God, is Lukas abusing him? Ewansiha had never got the impression that Lukas would be violent, and Sergio, who Ewansiha knew had good judgement, trusted Lukas. But really... How well did any of them know each other? They spent most of their time playing football and practising. There wasn't a lot of time for chatting and learning about each other.

"No. That's all right. I'll catch him tomorrow." Ewansiha turned to walk down the steps. He didn't think talking to Lukas was a good idea at the moment.

"Wait. What's your name? So I can tell him you stopped by."

"Tell him King stopped by. It wasn't anything important."

He dashed down the steps and jogged away. He didn't stop when he heard the kid yelling something. There was no way he could look Lukas in the face after seeing the bruises on the other guy's body. Not without demanding answers that he wasn't sure he wanted to know.

* * * *

"Good morning," Lukas greeted Xav as he walked into the kitchen to find him rummaging in the refrigerator. Xav looked up guiltily, but Lukas waved him back towards what he'd been doing. "We've gone over this. Eat when you're hungry, okay? I can afford to feed someone as skinny as you. Trust me." He walked over to join Xav at the appliance. "In fact, since we're both up early, why don't I make a cooked breakfast today? Put those eggs and the block of cheese on the counter for me, would you?" Lukas grabbed a pepper and an onion then found a package of sausage in the meat keeper.

"You know how to cook, huh?" Xav walked over and settled onto the stool at the counter to watch him closely as he pulled out the chopping board and a sharp knife.

Lukas smiled at his interest. "It's a good skill to have in life, especially when you like to eat." He placed the sausage in a skillet to start cooking then focused on preparing the vegetables. Xav watched his every move. "I'll teach you if you like," he casually offered.

Xav didn't respond right away so Lukas looked up at him in enquiry. He caught a sad, slightly confused expression that Xav immediately smoothed out.

"What's the frown for?" he asked the young man, who immediately looked away and shrugged.

He didn't press, not wanting to force the communication between them. He'd learnt even in a couple of days that Xav got defensive in a hurry when he felt uncomfortable with a topic—which included basically any reference to either the past or the future.

Lukas was grateful, though somewhat surprised, that Xav was still here. After he'd brought Xav home from the club two nights before, they'd gone round about Lukas' expectations and motivations for hours, with Xav believing the worst despite Lukas' assurances. Lukas had finally thrown his hands up and told Xav he could do whatever the hell he wanted and that he was going to bed because he had practice in the morning. He'd gone into his room, shut the door and settled down to sleep with his white-noise machine cranked up on high. He honestly hadn't thought Xav would still be there in the morning, and a cynical part of him had figured he might end up missing some valuables.

Yet when he'd come down yesterday morning, there Xav had been, sitting on the couch, not quite meeting Lukas' gaze. Lukas had been so damn relieved to see the young man still there that he'd probably been overly effusive in telling him to make himself at home, that he could come and go as he pleased and that he could have access to anything in the house, except Lukas' bedroom.

He'd left for practice yesterday certain that he'd come home to an empty house, but Xav had again stayed. Lukas had shopped while he'd been out and had brought home some inexpensive new clothes for him, unsure of what Xav had in his pack. He'd evidently been a bit optimistic on the sizes. The sweatpants he wore this morning were barely staying on his hips, though the length was a good fit. Xav had on what was apparently one of his own T-shirts, faded black with some kind of graphic design in white on it.

Lukas glanced down at Xav's bare feet, wondering if he should ask if the socks he'd bought had fitted. He noticed that one of Xav's big toenails was black, and not from Goth nail polish. Lukas had had his share of injuries there before and knew it was probably from getting tromped on. His heart clenched as he realised that, unlike with his experiences, it probably hadn't been accidental.

Which reminded him...

"I'd really like to take you to the doctor today." Though it was a necessary topic, Lukas braced himself for a negative reaction.

"Why?"

The response wasn't angry or upset, so Lukas began to cautiously hope that he could get Xav to go in. "I'd like to have you tested to make sure you don't have...anything that needs treatment, and also to look at your general health and physical well-being." He'd noticed some bruising and abrasions once he'd got a good look at Xav in decent lighting. He tended to move slowly, though whether that was from compensating for a hidden injury or just an affectation, Lukas didn't know.

Xav met his gaze solemnly and Lukas wished he knew what was going on behind those dark eyes. He felt helpless but incredibly protective of Xav, had from the start really. The worldly wise facade he showed the world was just that—a mask—and Lukas hoped that what he'd been through wasn't insurmountable when it came to settling back into the life of a normal teenager.

And how's he going to do that? Keep living here with you? Are you really ready to be 'the dad' to a teenager you don't even know?

Troubled, Lukas waited for Xav's response as he thought about the awful alternative—Xav back out on the street and picking up older men in the club. Why *couldn't* he let Xav stay with him? He had plenty of money and no one to spend it on, he lived alone and Xav had already proven that he was not going to be a disruptive housemate. At least, he hadn't been so far.

Maybe it was too early to know what the future would hold, but Lukas knew he'd be worried sick every day if Xav left now.

He decided to just put it out there. "Look, I know this is all happening really fast. And you don't have any special reason to trust me. But I care about what happens to you and I have plenty of room, and money enough not to worry about that sort of thing. I want you to stay here with me, long term, at least until you have somewhere else to go, even if that takes a couple of years. Consider me like a big brother or uncle or something. We'll get you back in school if you want, keep you safe and healthy and go from there. Okay?"

Xav's jaw dropped and his eyes got a bit misty. He looked incredibly young as he swallowed hard. "So I can just…live here with you? For real?"

"Of course you can."

"You're burning the sausages."

Lukas blinked at the abrupt change of topic, turned around with a curse and moved the skillet off the burner. They weren't actually burnt, but would be a bit overbrowned on one side. "Thanks. See? I obviously need someone around here to keep me in line." He pulled a second skillet out to sauté the vegetables in.

Xav gave the promising ghost of a smile. "Maybe if I stay you can teach me to cook. Though I haven't really seen you do much more than mangle the vegetables and burn the meat."

He gave Xav a mock look of outrage. "Trust me, I can cook. Just wait until you taste my eggs." He smiled inwardly as he began breaking eggs into a bowl.

"I, um… I hope I didn't get you in trouble. I answered the door last night."

Lukas paused in scrambling the eggs. Sometimes following Xav's conversations was like watching an old-fashioned pinball machine. "Oh? Who was it?"

"Big black guy—called himself...King, I think? You were sleeping. Sorry. Maybe I shouldn't have answered. I mean, it's not my house, but it's kinda automatic when someone knocks..." He trailed off.

Ewansiha had stopped by? "Did he leave a message?" Lukas asked. He wondered what he'd come by for and also what he'd thought of his guest's presence. Guess he'd have to explain...but then again, how could he tell his teammate that Xav had tried to pick him up in a gay club, and he'd decided to bring the teen home with him, even for totally innocent reasons?

"Nope. Just told me his name then ran off." Xav paused. "He looked really surprised to see me here so I hope he doesn't think anything bad is going on. I can tell him whatever you want me to."

"Don't worry about it. King's a really nice guy. I'm sure he didn't think anything of it." Though Xav's presence would definitely need to be addressed at some point. After breakfast, Lukas would call Sergio and figure out what, if anything, he should say to Ewansiha, and also find out where to take Xav to get tested. Plus, he'd spoken rashly about getting Xav back in school, but how could he accomplish that?

Lukas shook his head. Looked like he was going to be getting some schooling of his own—a crash course in being a 'parent'.

"Mind setting the table?" he asked Xav and smiled to himself when Xav groaned but slowly got up off the stool.

And so it begins...

Chapter Five

Lukas was feeling pretty good about life in general when he walked into the almost empty locker room to get ready for practice. He sang off-key under his breath to the last song he'd heard on the radio on the way there.

"You're in a good mood today." Sergio passed by him heading towards the door to the hallway, carrying a huge, black, boxy bag that looked heavy. Maybe some kind of electronic equipment, or a portable ultrasound?

"Need some help, honey?" he offered.

Sergio didn't even pause on his way out of the door. "Oops, you must have me mixed up with a damsel in distress. Wrong movie. This is the macho sports flick."

"Sorry!" he called, hoping that Serge was just being snarky and not truly offended. A bit chastened, he turned back towards his locker and, seeing movement out of the corner of his eye, noticed that Ewansiha was sitting on the bench across the room putting on his shin guards.

"Hey, King. Heard you stopped by last night." He unzipped his bag and started arranging his gear.

When no response came, he looked over at Ewansiha, who evidently hadn't heard him. He left his stuff and walked closer. "Hey, man, heard you came by. Just in the neighbourhood?"

Ewansiha flicked him a look but didn't acknowledge him in any other way, nor did he answer him. It was an obvious snub, and the contempt in that brief glance hit him right in the solar plexus. Lukas' good mood was now a thing of the past and his stomach began to roil. If anything, King had a reputation as a nice guy—even to assholes like Padraig—so why he was giving Lukas the cold shoulder after they'd had such a good day at practice yesterday could only mean one thing...

He saw Xav and must have figured out I'm gay. Fuck.

He wouldn't have pegged Ewansiha as being anything like Padraig, but such an abrupt about-face would only come if his entire opinion of Lukas had changed as the result of something he considered intolerable.

Lukas glanced around them, seeing that the locker room was starting to fill up, and rather than go anywhere with the conversation in front of all their teammates, he beat a hasty retreat, feeling sick to his stomach as he finished getting ready for practice without any further conversation with anyone.

Since he was done a few minutes early, he decided to try to rectify at least one encounter that had gone wrong and headed to Sergio's office. He wasn't inside when he knocked on the open door, so he tried the treatment room and found Sergio with his ass sticking out of a storage room, still wrestling with the bag he'd been carrying.

He quickly crossed the room. "If I offer you help again, it isn't because I think you're a girl—it's because it looks like you need an extra pair of hands."

Sergio sighed in relief as Lukas pressed up behind him in the narrow space and reached over him to help him manoeuvre the bulky item up onto the shelf. "Thanks. Sorry for being a bitch." He lightly wriggled his ass against Lukas and they both laughed as they backed out of the closet.

They turned around and the laughter died in Lukas' throat as he spotted Ewansiha looming in the doorway to the treatment room, glaring at them with narrowed eyes. Sergio appeared oblivious to the dark mood as he cheerfully greeted the other player. "King. Hop on up on the table and let's check the damage."

"Damage?" Lukas blurted out before he thought.

Sergio patted him on the shoulder. "Sorry, Lukas. You know I can't discuss details with you here." He glanced pointedly at the door. "Thanks for your help, but I have an appointment now."

Lukas was loath to leave Sergio alone with Ewansiha in the wake of his negative reaction to Lukas after seeing Xav at his house. That, plus his suspicious look when he'd caught Lukas and Sergio coming out of the closet...

Nice pun, by the way.

Fuck, the last thing he wanted was to have outed Serge, then have had to leave them alone together...

He didn't budge.

Sergio lifted an eyebrow at him. "Lukas?" He gestured to the door. "Can you excuse us?"

"Can I talk to you first?" He had to warn Sergio of Ewansiha's attitude.

"What the fuck? Fine!" Sergio threw his hands up then stomped out of the treatment room and straight into his office. He waited for Lukas to come in with barely concealed impatience then shut the door a bit harder than was necessary.

"Look, I just wanted to tell you about—"

"What the hell is with you?"

Their opening salvos clashed, so Lukas held up a hand in apology. "Let me explain?"

"Please do. You have two minutes."

Jeez, no pressure. "Okay. Um, well, I think that King knows"—he lowered his voice—"that I'm gay because he stopped by last night and Xav answered the door. Now today he won't even speak to me and he was giving me an evil look and then when we were coming out of the closet he looked suspicious and I didn't want to leave you alone with him if he's all pissed off and being a 'phobe. I mean, he's never been violent—even out on the field he never gets fouls, really—but he gave me the worst look, and I didn't want that to spill over onto you because—"

"Whoa!" Sergio's eyes were wide with astonishment. "Take a breath before you pass out."

"Well, you're the one who limited me to two minutes," he reminded him. "Anyway—"

Sergio grasped his upper arms and cut him off. "Honey, I have nothing to fear from Ewansiha, and neither do you. He is not a homophobe, not even close. He knows I'm gay and we're tight. So, if he's upset with you about something, it wouldn't have anything to do with that." He narrowed his eyes in thought. "Actually, if he saw Xav, he's probably pissed off because he thinks you're doing a teenager."

Lukas winced. That was even worse. "I've never even looked at Xav that way," he protested hotly. "Not even at the club. The only reason I talked to him was to keep him away from the others, and I got him out of there right away."

"I know that, but Ewansiha doesn't. I have no idea why he'd jump to the worst conclusion possible, but all it'll take to straighten this out is a simple conversation. Come on."

He grabbed Lukas' hand and tugged until he began to follow him under his own power. They left the office and Lukas turned the tables and pulled Sergio to a halt to whisper urgently, "I still don't want him to know I'm gay."

Sergio gave him a withering look then walked away into the treatment room. Lukas cursed under his breath and quickly followed.

Sergio waited until he'd entered then closed the door behind him. It appeared that Ewansiha's mood hadn't improved any while they'd been gone. It struck Lukas that he hadn't heard him say a word all day and rather than let Sergio take the lead, he jumped in.

"Look, I know you're pissed off at me about something, and since we were fine yesterday, it's probably something to do with my friend Xav staying at my house."

Ewansiha met his gaze calmly but didn't volunteer any information or change his icy expression. Sergio sighed loudly.

"Look, honey. Lukas is just trying to help the kid out by letting him stay there until he can figure out what to do. Nothing else is going on."

"Are you sure about that?"

"Yes. Why? What makes you think otherwise?" Sergio asked boldly.

Ewansiha didn't answer right away and, getting angry at the false accusations, Lukas prompted, "Tell me why you would think, after all the time we've been friends, that I would do anything bad or inappropriate to a sixteen-year-old kid. Huh? You really think that little of me?"

"I saw all his bruises. Someone's been abusing him—recently."

Lukas froze. "What bruises?"

Ewansiha gestured angrily all up and down his torso. "Ribs, upper arms, abdomen. He didn't turn around so I couldn't see his back, but he had his shirt off and he's so pale it was obvious as shit."

"And you think I did that?" Lukas couldn't move. He'd never felt so vilified. Even the few times he'd been on the receiving end of slurs for being gay had never had the effect that Ewansiha's low opinion had on him. He honestly thought he might throw up.

Ewansiha seemed to deflate somewhat. "God. No... Not really. I was just shocked he was there in the first place and then I started thinking, do any of us really know the other? What goes on behind closed doors? I...shouldn't have jumped to conclusions, but they were definitely really recent, and if he was staying with you..." He trailed off miserably.

Sergio cleared his throat. When Lukas glanced at him, he looked as though he'd been slapped. "Ewansiha... I was there two nights ago, the night that Lukas met Xav. He protected him, took him to a café and fed him then offered him a place to stay, no strings attached. The kid had been homeless and...doing risky things. So it was one of those situations that caused what you saw. Not Lukas. Never him. You trust me, don't you? Lukas would never hurt a soul."

Sergio pressed his lips together, obviously upset, either by the news of Xav's injuries or the idea that

Ewansiha could have suspected it of Lukas. Probably both.

Fuck it. Lukas moved to put his arm around him in comfort. He refused to look at Ewansiha, concentrating instead on Serge.

"Fuck. God, Lukas, I'm so sorry. I... I really had a hard time believing you might... But I couldn't think of any other..." Ewansiha sighed. "Looking back, I don't know why I jumped to that conclusion. I had a mental malfunction or something. Please forgive me." He groaned. "And here you were basically being a hero to the kid, and I treated you like a pervert or abuser. What the hell was I thinking?"

He seemed so profoundly upset and sorry that Lukas couldn't help but let go of his anger. Most of it, anyway. "It's okay, man. I'm not sure what I would have thought, so I guess I can't blame you for seeing something and drawing a conclusion." He frowned. "I wish I'd known about the bruises. Now I definitely need to get him to the doctor, today if possible, tomorrow at the latest."

Lukas looked at Sergio, who still looked poleaxed by the whole situation. "Can I talk to you about a few things after you're done with King?" He began backing towards the door, determined to give them their privacy for Ewansiha's session, whatever the problem was now. He hoped it wasn't anything serious.

Sergio blinked. "Oh...yeah, sure. About Xav?"

Lukas nodded then glanced briefly at Ewansiha, still uneasy with putting himself out there, before looking back at Serge. "Actually, let's talk later. Meet after skills?"

"Sure thing. Just find me when you're done."

"Lukas." Ewansiha's soft voice stopped Lukas in his tracks as he opened the door. "I'm really sorry."

He nodded without turning around. "I know. It's okay." He cleared his throat, striving for a more assured tone. "We're good." With that, he left the two men in the room and closed the door behind him. Part of him wanted to call Xav and demand to know the full extent of what had happened to him, and part of him was afraid of the answer.

He finally decided to wait and try to broach the subject in person when he got home. In the meantime, he needed to take his frustration and emotions out on the practice field.

* * * *

Ewansiha sneaked out of the sports medicine room like a dog with its tail tucked between its legs. *What the hell were you thinking last night? You idiot. Lukas would never do something like that. Sergio wouldn't be his friend if there was any hint that he'd abuse someone.*

Sergio hadn't said a word to him that didn't have to do with his knee. It hadn't been the most comfortable moment of his life, but Ewansiha had said he was sorry and had owned up to his mistake. He hoped Lukas would forgive him eventually for it.

He put his boots on, then tightened the laces. Wincing at the slight ache in his knee, Ewansiha knew the late night run hadn't been a good idea. Not only for what it had done to his possible friendship with Lukas, but because it had put more strain on his knee than he needed right now.

The doctors had told him that as long as he kept practising like he was, and doing the exercises they'd given him, he'd be back to a hundred per cent when the season started. Yet there were times when he didn't think that would ever happen.

"Quit your moping, and get out there," he muttered to himself as he jogged out onto the field where the rest of his teammates were waiting for him.

"Bit of a diva, aren't you, King? Keeping us out here waiting while you lollygag in the locker room," Padraig called out to him.

Ewansiha ignored him, used to being called a diva by his team captain. It was nothing new, so he started stretching, glad that he'd gone to see Sergio beforehand. No matter how angry the man might be at him, Sergio was a professional and would never take his anger out on Ewansiha.

Lukas jogged by, and Ewansiha met the man's cool blue eyes. His mother would be so ashamed of him for how poorly he'd treated Lukas. Damn! He knew what had short-circuited his brain last night—it was Silvia's request for his sperm. If she hadn't dropped that bomb on him at dinner, he would've never been out at that time, and would've never stopped by Lukas' house to talk.

With a shake of his head, he took off, catching up to Lukas easily. One thing Ewansiha could do, even with pain, was run. He loved running almost as much as he loved having sex. It was one of the reasons why he loved football so much. He got to run all over the field, chasing the ball and the other players.

The tightening of Lukas' shoulders was the only hint that the man knew Ewansiha was next to him. They ran around the field once in silence, then as they started their second lap, he couldn't take it anymore.

"I really am sorry about jumping to the wrong conclusion, Lukas," he apologised yet again.

Lukas grunted, then said, "We're good, man. I told you that. I'm not holding a grudge or anything."

Maybe not, but he could tell Lukas still wasn't happy with him. Ewansiha wished he could do or say something that would bring back the easy camaraderie they'd had before he had screwed things up. Finally, he reached out to grab Lukas' arm, jerking the man to a stop.

He didn't care what the others thought about the two of them standing there staring at each other. All he wanted was to see a smile back on Lukas' face, like there'd been before Ewansiha had acted like a jerk.

"Go ahead." He gestured at Lukas.

"Go ahead and what?" Lukas placed his hands on his hips, his chest heaving.

Ewansiha tried very hard to keep his attention on trying to reconcile with him, not imagining what it would be like to have Lukas panting under him while he took the man. His cock started to stiffen, and Ewansiha quickly got himself in control again. No need for anyone to know he was attracted to Lukas. It wouldn't be good for either of them.

"Go ahead and yell or punch me or something." Ewansiha braced for the impact of Lukas' fist in his face.

"Man, I told you we're good. Just leave me the hell alone today, and tomorrow we'll be right as rain." Lukas whirled around, then took off.

Letting him go, Ewansiha decided maybe he would play the injury card and get out of practising today. It wasn't going well, and he should've just never got out of bed. So for the first time in his entire career, Ewansiha went to his coach and told him a lie to be able to leave.

After showering and changing within twenty minutes, Ewansiha stalked out of the stadium, determined to go home. He was going to soak his painful knees in his hot tub, and maybe drown his sorrow in a gallon of Italian gelato. He indulged in desserts very rarely, and not at all while in training, but today just seemed like the day to do it.

His phone rang as he slid behind the wheel of his car. He engaged the hands-free setting, and answered it. "Kroenig."

"Hello, Ewansiha."

"Hey there, darling. How are you feeling today?" He smiled at Sil's voice. She might have thrown him off his game yesterday, but he still loved her.

"I'm feeling good. I set up an appointment for us with my doctor tomorrow. They'll take some of your sperm and run some tests. We'll know by the end of the day if you're a good candidate. Then the day after, he'll do what needs to be done to impregnate me."

His head spun, and he was glad he hadn't started driving anywhere. "Aren't we moving too fast, Silvia? I mean you just told me yesterday what you had planned. I haven't even had a chance to think about it."

She sighed. "I don't have a choice, King. We're coming up on the best time in my fertility cycle for us to try it. I won't have time over the next couple of months to try again, and we really want to start our family as soon as possible."

Fighting the urge to plug his ears with his fingers and say 'la-la-la' to drown out her words, Ewansiha admitted, "I'm not in the mood for this. I'm having a very crappy day, and I just want to go home and go back to bed."

"What's wrong? That doesn't sound like you." Her concern filled his heart with joy. At least he could count on her to support him.

"I made a complete ass of myself," he confessed, then went on to tell her about what he'd seen and what he'd thought Lukas had done. When he'd finished, he waited for her to tell him he was right to jump to those conclusions.

"You're an idiot, Ewansiha Ajani Kroenig."

Her bald statement shocked him.

"Why would you call me that?"

"Lukas Schulz isn't an abusive asshole or anything like that. He's a good guy, and I think you should take him flowers or grovel at his feet for a while because you are an idiot."

"How do you know Lukas?" He was heading for another freak-out. "How would you know he wouldn't do that? And besides, if he is gay, how was I not to know he wasn't sleeping with the kid?"

"Oh, for Christ's sake, Ewansiha." Her exasperation was clear in her tone. "I always thought you were so intelligent, but now I'm not so sure. What did you think of Padraig O'Leary the first time you met him? First reaction."

"Arrogant, closeted bastard who hates what he is so much he takes it out on other people."

"What about Paolo?"

"High-strung, super-talented diva who is more concerned about how he looks than how he plays. He's going to burn fast and furious, then plummet to the earth." And it was sad really, because Paolo had the talent to be one of the best that ever played football, but he wasn't going to last long enough.

She hummed, then asked, "Lukas Schulz."

"Talented kid. Has his act together, and knows what's important to do his job and play his role. He's not a hot-dogger or an attention whore. He's level-headed. Doesn't get into fights and is a generally good guy." He thumped his forehead on the steering wheel. "You're right. I'm an idiot."

"I am right. Now go home, eat your gelato and think about how to make it up to him." She laughed. "I'll text you the time for the appointment and where to meet me."

Silvia hung up before he could say anything else. After closing his eyes, he pinched the bridge of his nose. Yes, this had turned out to be one of the worst days in Ewansiha's life, and he was going home to lick his wounds. He'd figure out all the other bullshit later.

Chapter Six

"Do you seriously think I should bring him flowers or send him something?" Ewansiha held open the door of the high-rise where they were going to see Silvia's doctor. He had to ask her if she had meant what she'd said the day before. "I mean, Lukas isn't a girl. In fact, he's all man. Wouldn't he be insulted that I sent him flowers as an apology? Maybe I should just send him some whisky or beer or something."

Silvia shook her head. "If I didn't know any better, I'd think there wasn't a romantic bone in your body."

He watched her punch the call button for the lift, then asked, "What does being romantic have to do with it?"

Rolling her eyes, Silvia slid her hand into the crook of his elbow and leaned into his side while they waited. "Darling, like I said last night, you're the smartest man I know, but God, you can be dense sometimes."

"Then explain it to me." The lift doors opened, and he nodded politely to several people as they walked past them. Once the car was clear, he gestured for

Silvia to step in ahead of him. No one joined them, so he felt free to continue the conversation. "It's not like we're dating."

"I know you, King, and you'd like to be dating him." She winked and her grin held a hint of a leer to it as she pushed the button for the floor they needed. "Or maybe not dating, but you'd like to be doing him, that's for sure."

Not for the first time Ewansiha thanked God that his dark skin hid any signs of blushing. He scowled at his best friend. "I don't know what you're talking about."

She bumped their shoulders together. "Oh come on. You wouldn't be doing all of this and worrying about getting back into his good graces if you didn't like him, or weren't attracted to him."

"I can be attracted to him all I like, but it doesn't mean anything. He might not even be gay, no matter what rumours are circulating about Lukas."

"I think you could be pleasantly surprised if you give yourself a chance to find out." Silvia's cryptic statement brought another frown to his face.

The lift stopped, and he escorted Silvia out into a very posh lobby where several beautiful women and a few very good-looking men sat. Some of them were chatting, some were reading magazines.

He leaned over to whisper in Silvia's ear, "Are you sure this is a fertility doctor and not a plastic surgeon?"

Silvia gasped before slugging him in the biceps. "I can't believe you'd say that. Like I'd ever go see a plastic surgeon. This face and body are *au naturel*, my friend. I work hard to look this good."

"I didn't say you needed work or anything like that, but there isn't an ugly person in this lobby. Maybe he only takes on gorgeous clients, so his portfolio isn't filled with ugly children. Does the procedure come with a guarantee? Beautiful baby or your money back?" He kept his voice low, not wanting anyone to overhear him.

"Hush. Just shut up and sit over there." Silvia pointed to the corner where two chairs were set up in a rather intimate setting, considering they were at a doctor's office. "I'm going to check us in and get the paperwork you have to fill out."

"Yes, ma'am." He bowed slightly before doing what she had said. Smiling, he took his seat, then crossed his legs, wincing at the tightness in his knee.

Practice had been crazy that morning, and he'd had his own doctor's appointment an hour before this one, so he'd been excused from the afternoon session. To be honest, he'd rather have been at the stadium with the rest of the team. They were coming up on the first game of the season, and he needed more time getting back into shape after the surgery had forced him to take three months off. Maybe he'd go back after their appointment to do some more drills. He didn't need the other guys there for him to do it.

He loved people watching, so he studied the others in the room with him while he waited for Silvia to come back. He was the worst dressed out of all of them, and that made him chuckle softly. His jeans were worn in certain places and they bothered Silvia's high fashion sensibilities, which had been one of his goals. However, the jeans were comfortable, and big enough around the knees to hide the brace he'd been ordered to wear.

It was stupid that he had to hide it, but he didn't want any sports reporter seeing it and speculating on his health. Ewansiha hated all the gossip that was considered news nowadays. It had ruined the reputation of a lot of good athletes over the years.

"Why don't you throw those ragged things out?" Silvia sat next to him, her disdain for his jeans evident in the curl of her upper lip as she handed him a clipboard filled with papers.

"They're comfortable. I've finally got them broken in." He was used to the argument. Hell, if she had her way, Silvia would go through his entire closet and dress him in designer clothes only. He wasn't that vain. He wore top of the line suits when he went out on dates, or went to functions with her, but when it was just him, he dressed in jeans and T-shirts.

He grimaced as he started to fill in the lines.

She rested her hand on his knee, and her wide eyes met his when she felt the brace under the fabric. "Are you okay, Ewansiha? You haven't hurt yourself again?"

"No, honey." He covered her hand with his. "It's just precautionary. The doctors want to make sure I don't twist it or anything like that. I have to wear it until the first game, then I can take it off."

Her concern eased a little, but he could tell she was still worried. Ewansiha didn't want to talk about his knee anymore. It was a frustrating topic at the best of times. He returned their conversation to what she'd said earlier.

"What did you mean by I'd be pleasantly surprised if I made a move on Lukas?"

Silvia met his gaze, and he could see the moment she accepted the change in topic. "I was just saying you need to put yourself out there a little more, and if you did, you might discover things aren't quite what they seem."

"Are you saying Lukas really is gay?" He kept his voice low, knowing that if anyone overheard them, their conversation would be leaked to the media in seconds. Hell, he wouldn't put it past someone to record it for a quick buck.

She shrugged. "I'm not saying anything really. All I'm saying is that you need to get out there and find someone, Ewansiha. I don't care if it's a woman or a man. Just as long as it's someone who loves you for all the wonderful things you are and can give a person."

Cupping her face with his hands, he leant forward to place a kiss on her lips. There wasn't any passion in it, simply the knowledge of caring and love between two best friends. When he settled back in his chair, she blinked tears out of her eyes.

"Thank you for caring, Silvia," he told her.

"You're welcome. Next to Wendy, you're my best friend, and I want you to have what she and I have together. You deserve it." She entwined their fingers together, then rested against his shoulder as best she could without sitting in the same chair as him.

"So you think I should put myself out there, and take a chance on Lukas?" Ewansiha rubbed his thumb over her knuckle as he thought about Lukas. There wasn't any doubt that he was attracted to the blond, far more than he'd ever been to any of his other teammates.

She nodded. "I do. You told me he seems really close with Sergio, and that tells me he doesn't have a problem with gay men. So even if he's straight, he's more than likely not going to freak out on you if you ask him out."

That was true. He'd seen how tight Lukas and Sergio seemed together, and while Sergio never spoke about it around the team, there really wasn't any way he could hide the fact that he was gay. *Thank God, no one's harassed him about it.* Ewansiha had at least noticed that, and if he ever found out that someone had, he might lose his legendary cool and beat that person's ass.

"I'll think about it, and I'm not sending him flowers. Maybe if we were dating, I'd do it, but flowers seem too personal at the moment."

"You could just ask him out for a drink as an apology, then see where it goes from there," she suggested.

He nodded. "I might do that. Hell, even if he's not gay, I still want us to go back to the way we were. I think he could be a really good friend, if I manage not to insult him again."

Silvia's laughter rang out like a chime, and Ewansiha saw envy on the faces of the men in the room. Smiling, he decided to change the subject again, having made up his mind to ask Lukas out for drinks the first chance he got. He questioned her about the shoot she was heading back to when she left Germany.

They chatted for a while as she caught him up on her schedule, and what Wendy was doing as well. Ewansiha wasn't as close to Silvia's partner as he'd like to be, but they'd barely had time to get to know each other between their busy lives.

"Do you think maybe during my break, you, Wendy and I could go to the Islands for a vacation? I'd love to get to know Wendy better since she's going to be one of the mothers of my child."

"That's so weird."

He shot her a glance. "Really? I don't think my request is weird."

She giggled. "It is because Wendy kind of made the same suggestion this morning when we talked. We both have a month open at the end of December, and you'll have a break in the season by then. We could go to your place, and just relax."

A nurse came into the waiting room and called Silvia's name. Since she didn't let go of Ewansiha's hand when she stood, he was forced to rise as well.

"You're coming with me," she murmured to him as they walked across the floor to where the lady held the door open.

Her grip on his hand was so tight he thought she might break his fingers, so it wasn't like he could do anything except accompany her. He didn't want to hurt her to get away.

Let's face it. You were going to do this from the moment she told you she wanted children. You'd do anything for her.

And that was the honest truth. He'd give Silvia his sperm or his kidney. Hell, he'd probably give her his heart if she needed it.

* * * *

Half an hour later, they walked out of the building, holding hands. Silvia glowed with happiness at the news they'd received. She'd be having the procedure tomorrow to try to get her pregnant, and if it didn't work this time, she'd be back next month to do it again.

Somehow Ewansiha had a feeling that the process usually didn't go this fast, but when you had the money, you could speed everything up if you wanted to. Silvia was so eager to have a baby, and he'd guess he'd pay any amount to give her the chance to have one.

When they stopped on the sidewalk, she whirled around to throw her arms around his neck. He wrapped her up in a tight hug, then lifted her off her feet to swing her in a circle. As she laughed, she gave him a quick kiss.

After setting her back down, he grinned. "Are you happy, Silvia?"

"Very. If things go right, I could be a mother in nine months." She hugged herself in happiness. "And you'll be a father."

"That will take a little more getting used to," he admitted, still not entirely sure how he felt about a baby bearing his DNA being out in the world.

"It'll be fine. Now I have to go call Wendy, then I have a meeting with a designer that wants to use me in his ad campaign."

Ewansiha flagged down a cab for her, then kissed her on the cheek before she climbed in. "Call me when the results come in, and if I can, I'll come back with you for the procedure tomorrow."

"All right. Take care, Ewansiha, and I love you," she called out, then shut the cab door.

He headed to the garage where he'd parked his car. Going back to the stadium was next on his list of things to do. He would get in some extra practice, only he'd wear the brace since the doctors had told him to. At least regular practice was over with, so there might not be a lot of his teammates around. He really didn't want any of them seeing him like that.

Ewansiha had worked hard on building an image of being strong and invincible. His knee injury last year had put a crack in it, but he'd done his best to repair it and he would keep doing whatever he needed to make sure no one ever saw him as weak.

After he got to his car and turned the key, he pulled out of the garage to head home. His phone began blaring Sergio's ringtone. He answered the call on Bluetooth.

"Hey, Sergio. What's up?"

"Where have you been? I think you're ignoring my calls." Sergio sounded like he was pouting. "I'm not mad at you anymore."

Some tension he hadn't even known he was carrying disappeared. He hadn't realised how much he relied on Sergio's good opinion of him.

"I'm glad to hear that. I was at the doctor's, so I had the ringer off." He hadn't wanted to be interrupted while with Silvia. "What can I do for you?"

"I want you to go out dancing with me tonight. You haven't been out for a while, and I think you need to relax some more." Sergio sounded like dancing would fix all of his problems and Ewansiha knew better.

"I'm not sure, Sergio, unless you want to meet at one of the regular clubs."

Sergio never wanted to dance at the straight clubs. He wanted to go to the gay ones, so he had a better chance of picking someone up.

"Hell no. We're going to The Gypsy. I'll meet you there at nine, and don't think about chickening out. No one's going to instantly think you're gay just because you're there. Lots of straight people go to The Gypsy."

Sergio hung up before Ewansiha could either protest or say yes. He shook his head then continued home. Maybe Sergio was right—maybe he did need to let off some steam. He just had to figure out what to wear that would be comfortable, but help disguise him as well.

Chapter Seven

Lukas looked around the crowded waiting room of the clinic but didn't see any open seats. Maybe by the time they'd checked in something would have opened up. He and a very quiet Xav waited in line behind an obviously homeless old man with a horrible cough.

He second-guessed his decision to bring Xav here instead of to his own doctor's office, but Sergio had had a point—it was good for Xav to know that there were options for medical care he could walk into at any time, just in case he didn't stick around. Plus, they did fast and low-cost testing without an appointment.

While they waited, he wondered how Ewansiha's doctor's appointment for his knee had gone. If they'd been at Lukas' doctor's office, he might have even run into him there, since they had different doctors in the same office. Things had still been a bit awkward between them at the morning practice, but really, they'd been too busy to do more than nod to each other. And Ewansiha had taken the afternoon off. Lukas had chosen to leave the afternoon practice early, which he'd been able to do without any hassle, rather than miss one altogether.

When it was their turn at the window, Lukas placed his hand lightly on Xav's back to usher him forward. "He needs to be tested."

"Any other health concerns you need to be seen for today?"

"No," Lukas answered for him. He would definitely make an appointment with his own physician as soon as possible for anything else. He had private insurance for himself, though he wasn't sure how that would work with Xav being a minor. Was he still on his parents' coverage? He didn't think they could just stop it, though Xav might not want the information getting back to them. He'd have to find out. Meanwhile, he could just pay full cost if necessary.

"Fill out the top half of the sheet as best you can. If you don't have a current address, leave it blank. When you're done, bring back the clipboard to me and have a seat to listen for your name to be called."

Lukas nodded his thanks and led Xav over to an open bit of wall where they could at least stand without being in front of anyone. They had to dodge around a couple of kids heedlessly playing tag. The harried-looking mother—easy to spot since they all looked strikingly alike—was busy trying to soothe a squalling infant.

He tried to tune everything out and focus on Xav, who knelt down next to him to fill out the form. When he reached the address section his pen hesitated, and Lukas bent down to slowly tell him his. After a brief pause, Xav began writing furiously to fill it in. They did the same for the phone number, using Lukas' home phone.

Shoot. I should probably get him a cell phone. They weren't that expensive to add onto a current plan. He made a mental note to swing in to his provider's storefront, maybe on the way home…

Xav had got to the part about health coverage and looked up at Lukas. "I don't know if I…"

"Leave it blank. It's just a panel test, and only fifteen euros. I can pay that."

"I'll pay you back."

Lukas grimaced. Xav kept a running total of costs he believed he'd incurred, which made Lukas contrarily proud and irritated. "Xav, we've talked about this. Please don't worry about it."

Xav gave him a stubborn look and looked back down at the form. He finished the sections they'd been told to complete and glanced up at Lukas before standing and walking by himself over to the window. After a brief wait, he handed the clipboard back to the woman then returned to Lukas' side.

He shifted every few moments, and Lukas supposed that if they'd been sitting, his knee would have been bouncing. With his slight frame clad in somewhat baggy jeans and a hoodie, his face clean-scrubbed, he looked appallingly young to be on his own.

Well, he's not on his own anymore, Lukas thought fiercely. He wondered what his own parents would think about him mentoring the young throw-away. He would hope that they'd be supportive—maybe he should call his mom to let her know? She didn't completely understand Lukas' orientation, but she still loved him. She'd likely go straight into mothering mode. He got the feeling that many of her difficulties with his being gay stemmed from knowing she would never be a grandma, since Lukas was an only child.

Once it looked like Xav would be staying long term, he'd broach the subject of a visit from her and Dad.

Lukas realised there were a lot of things piling up under the 'if he stays' category. "Hey, Xav, can I ask you something before they call you back?"

Xav went still then slowly nodded. "Sure. What is it?" His apprehension was evident. Lukas hoped that someday soon he'd gain more confidence.

"Are you going to stay with me? For good? When we talked about it the other day, you asked if that's what I wanted you to do, which I do, but you never told me if that's what *you* want." Lukas watched Xav's profile closely. "I don't want to pressure you. I'm just tired of wondering every time I go somewhere whether you'll be there when I get home," he confessed honestly.

Xav met his gaze then, his eyes wide with surprise. "I…" He appeared to gather his thoughts. "Yeah. I'll stay."

"You *want* to?" Lukas stressed. "Because I want you to, but you have to want it too."

Xav nodded, then, seeming to realise that Lukas needed to hear the words, said in a clear voice, "I want to stay with you."

"Good." Lukas gave Xav a quick hug.

"Xavier M," was called out by a woman in white at the door by the check-in area.

He released Xav who took a couple of steps forward then turned back to look at Lukas. Fear surfaced briefly in his eyes. Lukas wasn't entirely sure whether they'd let him come in with him or not, but he wouldn't let Xav cross the room alone if he needed support. He strode quickly to catch up with Xav, whose relief was plain to see.

The door was held for them and they passed through into a busy hallway where Xav was weighed and his height noted. Then they were led into an exam room. Lukas kept expecting his presence to be questioned, but the technician or nurse—whatever she was—basically ignored him. She asked Xav a few questions from his form to confirm his identity—Müller was his last name, the first time Lukas had heard it. She took his temperature and blood pressure but didn't reveal the outcomes.

Finally the woman looked directly at Lukas. "For privacy reasons, we'll need you to step outside the door while the doctor is with him." He nodded his understanding and she instructed Xav, "There's a gown there behind you. Please take off your shirt only and put on the gown with the opening in the front." She left them alone in the room.

Xav didn't make any move to take off his shirt and Lukas knew he was probably trying to avoid revealing the bruising Ewansiha had noticed. He decided to make it easier on him. "I'll go out so you can get ready."

Xav looked embarrassed and relieved at the same time. "I'm sorry."

"Don't be. It's okay," he tried to reassure him. "I'll be right outside when you're done or if you need me." He felt ridiculously like he was abandoning him instead of just stepping out of the room, but made sure his expression was confident as he opened the door and gave Xav one last smile before closing it behind him.

The hallway wasn't exactly conducive to standing around in, but there was a chair right across the hallway by the scale they'd used, so he sat there, trying to stay out of the way of the patients and staff hurrying along.

At last, a short, older woman with salt and pepper hair in a ponytail, wearing a white lab-style coat, approached the room and lifted the chart from the slot by the door. She flipped it open and scanned it briefly then caught his eye. "Are you waiting for someone?"

"Yes, Xavier." He indicated the room, a bit uncomfortable under her intense gaze.

She appraised him. "Relative?"

"Friend," he corrected quickly, wanting to remain as truthful as possible since her focus seemed to brook no deception.

She nodded then without further discussion knocked on the door of the room and entered when bidden. "Hello, Xavier—I'm Doctor Mendez," was all he heard before the door closed. Try as he might, he couldn't hear anything else.

He waited impatiently, having to move out of his seat eventually when someone else came along needing to be weighed.

Finally, after what seemed like forever, the door opened and Dr Mendez came out, without the chart. She gave him an assessing look that he suffered as best he could without betraying his nervousness. He knew he didn't have anything to be scared of, but he'd never really felt comfortable with doctors, and with Xav's history, he didn't know whether they'd think anything wrong was going on.

She walked down the hall to the nurses' station and checked something that was printing out. After she had ripped it off, she signed it, handed it to another staff member, then she came back towards Lukas.

"He'd like you to come in for the next part," she said as she knocked on the door.

Lukas preceded her into the room. Xav's eyes were locked on him the minute he appeared and he looked pathetically glad to see him. Lukas knew he should probably keep his distance in front of the doctor, but that gaze pleaded with him and he ended up going to give him a brief but firm hug anyway before standing off to the side.

"They... They have to take blood. With a needle." Xav was as pale as a ghost.

"Well, yes, you knew we were coming here to get you tested, right? I thought you knew it was a blood test."

Xav shook his head rapidly. "I guess I didn't think about it."

Lukas walked the couple of steps back to his side. "It'll be fine. It'll sting a bit but not too bad. My advice?" He paused with Xav hanging on his every word. "Just don't look. And...maybe you can lie down while they do it?" This was directed at the doctor, who stood nearby listening to their conversation.

She nodded. "That might be best."

Xav immediately lay back and she smiled gently. "The phlebotomist isn't here to do the draw yet. You can stay sitting up until she comes. In the meantime, do you have any questions for me before I go to my next patient?"

Lukas covered for Xav as he quickly sat back up, looking embarrassed. "When will Xav get the results?"

"They're usually ready in about thirty minutes. So you can either stay in the waiting room and we can call you back in to give you the results, or you can call in and give us a code and we can have a counsellor give you the results over the phone."

He thought quickly. "If we ran a fast errand and came back, would that be okay?" He saw Xav look at him with a more normal expression, as though his curiosity had partially overcome his fear, or maybe he was just drawing strength from Lukas being by him.

"That would be fine. Check in at the desk when you're back, then you'll just have to wait for the next available counsellor." She looked between him and Xav then addressed the young man, "I would recommend doing as we discussed, but it's your choice." She glanced at Lukas again then gave a genuine-looking smile for the first time. "You're a lucky young man, you know."

Xav gave her a nod then looked at Lukas gratefully. "I know."

She left the room and, as they waited for the person who would do the blood draw, Xav looked at him seriously. "Can I ask you something?"

Lukas braced himself. "Sure."

"What errand? Where are we going?"

He burst out laughing then tried to tone it down as there was a knock on the door. A young woman in scrubs came in carrying a tray with vials and a syringe. Xav's laughter cut off immediately and he lay down like he'd been shot, eyes closed.

Lukas bit his lip to try not to laugh. He leaned over and patted Xav's shoulder. "It has something to do with a cell phone, but that's all I'm going to say." Xav's eyes popped open and he grinned at Lukas then glanced at the woman preparing the items. Lukas continued, "Just have to get through this and we'll hit the store down the street while we wait for the results. 'Kay?"

Xav closed his eyes again. "'Kay. Let's do this."

* * * *

On their way home, Lukas watched Xav out of the corner of his eye, pleased with how the day had gone. The huge worry of whether Xav had contracted anything had been alleviated, Xav had confirmed that he was planning to stay with Lukas indefinitely and he'd been thrilled to get a new cell phone. Lukas felt better knowing he was just a quick phone call or text away.

"So, is it okay to ask what it was the doctor meant at the end there? When she recommended that you do something?"

Xav grimaced and shrugged. "She just thought that I should let my parents know I'm okay. I mean, not say where I am if I don't want to, but just that I'm fine." He cleared his throat. "She asked me a lot of questions about you, whether you had done anything to me and if I felt safe in your house. Said she'd get me help and that I didn't have to go with you if I didn't want to."

Lukas gripped the steering wheel hard. It was difficult hearing that, though he understood that she had just been trying to give Xav options, in case Lukas hadn't been a good person.

"But I told her…um…how we met and how you were only ever respectful and nice to me. That you treat me like a kid brother. In a good way, I mean. Not like my real big brother did." He waved his hand, and Lukas let that pass. One day he'd get the full story from him. "Anyway," he rushed on, "I said that you were probably the best person I've ever met and she said I really lucked out that night. And I know I did. I wasn't always so lucky and… Well, the guy the night before you, he…" Xav trailed off as Lukas turned down their street, his heart aching.

"I didn't want to show you the bruises, but I don't even care about those. That was pretty stupid, making you leave, not even taking my shirt off."

"It wasn't stupid at all, Xav. And you have the right to your privacy, same as anyone."

Xav sat up a bit straighter as they pulled into the drive and Lukas pressed the button to open the garage door. "Thanks for...everything. And the phone too." He bounced once in the seat. "I missed having a phone so much. I've already programmed your number in. I memorised it, and look—I found a picture of you online for the profile pic." He showed Lukas a photo of him seemingly hovering in mid-air, about to strike the ball.

He parked and they went inside. Lukas heard his phone ringing and hurried to pick it up before it went to voicemail. "Hello?"

"Are you ignoring my texts?"

Lukas toed off his shoes and kicked them towards the garage door. "Hey, Serge—no. I didn't even hear... Oh. Crap, sorry. I turned down the volume at the doctor's office and forgot to turn it back on."

"That's the second time I've heard that today! What? Was there an excuse of the day thing on the radio I didn't hear about?" A sarcastic *humph*. "Anyway, I want you to come out with me tonight since we never did get a chance to dance the other day before you were rescuing your lost lamb."

"Tonight? Um..." He looked over at Xav who was unabashedly listening to his side of the convo. He nodded and flapped his hands as if to say *okay, go.* "Sure, why not?"

"Great. I'll meet you back at The Gypsy then, and try not to leave with any more special projects before I get there. In fact, no — don't meet me. I'll pick you up at nine."

"Wait, I'll just" — the phone disconnected and he pulled it away from his ear — "drive myself."

Xav started laughing. "I like Sergio. He's a bossy little guy."

"Don't ever let him hear you call him bossy. Or little. You sure you'll be okay tonight on your own?"

Xav gave him the eyebrow and his usual eye roll before grabbing an apple and taking a huge bite. "I'll be fine, Dad," he said sarcastically around the mouthful of fruit. "Sheesh."

Lukas didn't miss the slight smile as Xav turned away. No matter how much Xav protested, Lukas could tell a part of him relished being cared for. And he'd do everything he could to encourage that, to allow him to regain some of his youth that had been snatched away from him so coldly.

So that was settled. Now to figure out what to wear...

Chapter Eight

Nodding to the security guard, Ewansiha slipped into the main area of The Gypsy from behind the bar. Knowing the owner gave him the ability to come and go without having to stand in line or enter through the front door. Too many chances of getting a photo snapped of him, and no matter what Sergio said, there were those who'd jump on the 'he's gay' bandwagon, and Ewansiha wasn't ready for that.

He pulled out his phone as he stood at the end of the bar, then texted Sergio to let him know that he was there, and where he was. The bartender approached, and he asked for an unopened bottle of water. No drinking for him tonight. He wasn't going to risk getting drunk and doing something stupid in the middle of a crowded club.

"I thought you were going to stand us up."

Us? Ewansiha whirled around to see Sergio behind him, but it was the sight of Lukas standing next to his friend that shocked him. He felt his jaw drop, then shut it when Sergio cleared his throat.

"I came like you told me to, Sergio." Ewansiha held out his hand to Lukas. "Lukas. Good to see you."

They shook hands, and he had to smile at the hat and sunglasses the other man wore. Looked like he was trying to hide same as Ewansiha was. Ewansiha had chosen to wear a fedora, a black T-shirt that fitted him like a glove and black leather pants. He wore glasses, but they weren't shades. They were plain, yet they managed to disguise his looks, just like Superman's glasses did.

"I wanted to ask you at practice this morning about your knee. I hope it's doing all right." Lukas gestured towards Ewansiha's leg.

He shrugged. "It's doing fine. It'll be a hundred per cent by the time the first game comes around. Do you want a drink?"

He knew what Sergio would want, so he flagged down another bartender to order for his friend, then glanced back at Lukas, who asked for water. He grinned at the other man, happy to know he wasn't going to screw up his training by getting trashed then having to deal with a hangover the next day.

Being a veteran on the team, he'd seen a lot of talented guys come and go because they couldn't deal with the fame and everything that came with it. It was good to see that Lukas had a handle on things.

After handing out the drinks, he motioned to an out of the way table his friend had set up for him when he'd come to the club. Ewansiha could still see the dance floor and the writhing bodies that filled it, but the shadows hid him so he didn't have to worry about people spotting him.

So far he'd been lucky that not many photos of him had appeared in the tabloids, but he knew the day would come when someone would get a photo they had to share with the world. He just had to brace himself for that. He wasn't sure how Silvia dealt with the paparazzi.

"How was the rest of practice today? The coach run you ragged?" He sipped his water, not looking at Lukas because he'd end up staring, and he didn't want to be obvious about his interest. At least not at the moment.

"Seriously? You're going to talk shop while we're in a club with pumping music and hot guys?" Sergio curled his lip in annoyance with Ewansiha.

"Well, you were the one who invited me, Sergio. You know I don't dance, and even if I did, I can't do that right now." Ewansiha had left his brace at home, not wanting to ruin the line of the pants, and that decision was something he could blame on Silvia.

Sergio took one sip of his drink, then set it on the table. After standing, he held out his hand to Lukas. "Come on then. If King isn't going to dance with me, you are. I want to shake my ass and you're going to help me with that as well."

"I'm not sure I can help you shake your ass, Sergio," Lukas quipped as he joined Sergio next to the table. "How about I just dance near you until I'm pushed out of the way by your adoring fans like usual?"

Well, that sounds like Lukas has been dancing with Sergio before. Ewansiha watched them walk away, his gaze zeroing in on Lukas' firm ass covered by form-hugging, dark jeans. He clenched his hands, fighting the urge to chase after him and grab handfuls of those tight globes.

Instead of pushing their way through the crowd to the middle of the floor where Sergio usually danced, the pair stayed on the edges closest to Ewansiha. At times, it was almost like they were dancing for him alone, and Ewansiha's cock certainly seemed to like that idea.

He took a big swallow of water while pushing the heel of his hand down on his erection. *No thinking about them together. You're not going to be able to walk right when you leave here.* He'd never felt this level of attraction for any man, not even Sergio. Yet all he wanted right now was to grab both men, pull them into the bathroom, and kiss them.

As strange as it might have seemed, he'd never had a fantasy of a threesome. He already knew what Sergio tasted and sounded like during sex. Now he sat at his table, watching Lukas and Sergio dance, wrapped in each other's arms, and he couldn't help wondering what Lukas' skin would taste like under his tongue. What kind of sounds did the man make while being fucked? If Lukas was gay, which was starting to seem more and more likely, was he a bottom, a top or a switch?

"Hey, man, can I get your autograph?"

Tensing, he turned to see a man standing next to the table with a grin on his face. One of the security guards was already moving towards him, and he just had to try to convince the man Ewansiha wasn't who he thought he was.

"Why would you want my autograph, dude? I'm nobody." Ewansiha shifted slightly, leaning back into the shadows.

"Oh I know who are. You're King Kroenig. Totally awesome that you feel comfortable enough to hang out here, but you should be careful. Not everyone will be as understanding. They might think you're one of us."

Before he could respond, the bouncer was there to urge the kid to keep moving back into the crowd. *Shit!*

Ewansiha let his head drop back against the cushion of the booth, then thumped it again. *Why did life have to be so complicated?*

He'd love to jump up and say he was bi, and slept with guys as well as women. But nothing in the football community reassured him that they would accept him if he did say it.

He pushed back into the corner of the booth, hoping no one else approached him.

"Uh-oh," Sergio murmured in his ear. Lukas opened his eyes to look down at Serge, though he kept moving to the beat of the music. Serge was straddling his thigh and they were about as close as two guys could be without lube being involved.

"What's wrong, honey?"

"King's got company."

Lukas turned them on the floor so he could see towards their booth, but all he saw was the bouncer he'd seen on their way in walking away from the corner.

"Well, not anymore. But looks like someone possibly recognised him. Good thing Metzger was paying attention." Sergio slid his hand down Lukas' ass and gave a squeeze before shifting away. "We should probably get him out of here. He's a lot more recognisable than you are, and he hates..." Sergio trailed off.

"Hates what?" Lukas put his hand on Sergio's lower back to stay together as they moved through the crowd back to where Ewansiha was sitting.

Sergio sighed. "Hates the idea of being thought of as gay." Lukas bristled a bit and Sergio, who seemed totally in tune with his every mood, cautioned, "Down, boy. He's not like Padraig, by any means. He just wants to live in peace and finish out his career without drama."

What exactly did that mean? Was Sergio saying he *was* gay? Or that he didn't want to be mistaken for gay because his friends were? They'd reached the table, and Lukas could already tell they'd be leaving in a minute. King was slouched down, trying to blend into the booth.

"Come on, big guy. Let's head out." Sergio took control and tugged on Ewansiha's arm until he carefully stood, still looking stiff no matter how optimistic he was about his knee.

"Where to?" Lukas asked as they walked closely together towards the bar. Metzger saw them coming and opened the drop leaf to let them back, then Ewansiha led the way through towards what was evidently the rear entrance of the club.

"We'll go to... Oh. Can't go to yours with the kid there. King's it is," Sergio proclaimed. "I drove so we'll meet you there."

Lukas waited for Ewansiha to object to Sergio's high-handedness, but instead he laughed as they walked out into the cooling night air.

"Whatever you say, honey."

Lukas grinned at the sound of 'his' nickname for Sergio on King's lips. At the corner, they went one direction and King the other. As they approached Sergio's car, Lukas' curiosity got the best of him. "Have you been to King's house before?"

Sergio gave him a smirk. "Yes."

"Huh." Lukas waited as Serge popped the locks then climbed in. Ewansiha was notoriously private and didn't really socialise with the other guys on the team except for official functions and command performances.

Sergio bounced into his seat, started his Audi and quickly took off into traffic. Lukas listened to the music Sergio cranked up and braced himself as best he could against the sudden lane changes and fast turns.

He decided to see how Xav was doing and finally managed to text him.

Everything okay?

Yes. Just chillin came back a second later.

"That Xav?" Sergio asked.

"Yeah. I got him a cell phone today and he must have it glued to his hand." They laughed and Lukas continued, "It was a lot of fun seeing him so excited about it."

"Yeah, poor kid. Man—he sure hit on the right guy."

Lukas winced. "Don't remind me. Ah well, at least that got rid of my semi hard-on." He gave Serge a wink. "Sexy dancer. And after all, it's not like we can sneak into King's guest room for a quickie."

Sergio leered at him and Lukas had to restrain himself from grabbing the wheel. "You don't think so? Hmm, too bad. I was kind of looking forward to a little time in his hot tub with you...and him."

Lukas had no comeback for that. His heart nearly stopped at the thought of Sergio and Ewansiha in a hot tub, droplets of water running down their naked bodies...

So much for getting rid of my hard-on.

They soon pulled up in front of a gated house and Sergio rolled down his window and entered a pass code.

"Really? You know his security code?" Lukas stared at Sergio as the gates slowly swung open. He drove through them and up a curved driveway.

"Yes. I told you I've been here before."

Lukas was beginning to get the picture and he wasn't entirely sure he liked what he was seeing. Far from being intolerant or homophobic, it seemed Ewansiha liked to walk on the wild side...in private. He hated the thought of Sergio being used by someone who didn't own being gay. Lukas may keep his private life private, but at least he copped to who he was with the people in his life who counted. And last Lukas knew, King was dating a woman...and before that, another woman. And so forth.

Sergio got out of the car and Lukas reluctantly followed suit. They walked to the towering front entrance and Sergio didn't bother to knock or ring, but instead opened the unlocked front door and strode in like he owned the place.

He held the door open for Lukas. "Well, come on in. Don't be shy."

Lukas wished he'd driven or that he had the guts to just tell Sergio they were leaving—now—but instead he followed him into the house.

"Honey, I'm home!" Sergio called out, laughing, then made a beeline for the vaulted living area and into an arched passageway that looked like it led to a kitchen.

"Hi, guys." Ewansiha's voice came from above and Lukas looked up to see him standing at the railing of the upper floor hallway. "I'm just getting changed. Make yourselves at home."

"Looks like Sergio already did," Lukas answered and Ewansiha smiled at him. Lukas felt the impact of that carefree smile all the way to his toes. God, was that what a real smile from the man looked like? Ewansiha disappeared from view into a doorway and Lukas was left wondering at the revelation that everywhere else but here, King had a game face on.

No wonder Sergio had been so insistent that they come here. Somehow the guy always knew how to make people feel good. King had been uncomfortable at the club, so he'd made sure they came somewhere he knew King would be able to be himself.

Lukas was looking forward to meeting the real Ewansiha.

He wandered slowly towards where Sergio had gone, looking around at the expensive yet welcoming house and its warm decor and furnishings. When he got to the kitchen, he wasn't in the least surprised to find Sergio clad in only his club pants, dancing to music he had turned on from a radio on the counter while mixing what looked like margaritas, or maybe mojitos, in a pitcher.

When Sergio spotted him, he gave him a sexy smile and moved towards him, hips swivelling to the beat of the music. Lukas welcomed him into his arms and they went right back to how they'd been dancing together at the club. After only a minute or so, Sergio started to impatiently tug at his shirt, trying to pull it out of his pants.

"It's not fair that I'm the only one wearing skin," he murmured in his ear and Lukas' cock began to respond to the promise in that voice.

He allowed Sergio to work the shirt free then he took the hem and slowly pulled it over his head before taking him back into his arms. There was something about the touch of their bare chests that amped things up considerably…

At least, that's what he thought until he felt the touch of another bare chest along his back a moment before he was wrapped in Ewansiha's long arms and yanked back against him.

The first ever touch between them sent Lukas' libido skyrocketing.

Lukas' embrace of Sergio brought him along for the ride, and the three of them began moving together in a synchronicity that seemed almost choreographed. It hit him suddenly that he was dancing in a man-wich that included King, his 'straight' fantasy man and teammate.

"I thought…" he started then stopped as Sergio's eyes warned him not to break the spell. "I thought…you said you couldn't dance."

Ewansiha's deep voice rumbled in his ear, sending shockwaves straight to his cock, "I said I *don't* dance. Which is true when I'm at a club. But in private…" He rolled against Lukas' ass in a sexy grind. "I can be persuaded. Especially when I find a party going on without me in my kitchen."

Sergio laughed and kept up an increasingly erotic pressure against Lukas' growing erection. The Spaniard knew how to use his assets well and he could dance like a stripper. Lukas kept a loose grip on Sergio's hips and looked down into his flirty dark eyes, but all of his focus was on the feel of Ewansiha's firm body moving behind him in a teasing parody of sex.

He groaned as that sent a slew of mental images rampaging through his head. His nipples hardened and he rested his head back against Ewansiha's broad shoulder. Used to being the bigger guy in most of his past pairings, it was a novel feeling. He closed his eyes…

And a chill hit his overheated skin along the front as Sergio pulled out of his arms then began to strip off his pants right there in the kitchen.

Lukas and Ewansiha came to a mutual halt to watch the impromptu and very short striptease. Soon every inch of Sergio's caramel-coloured skin was on display, his cock hanging heavily against his reddish sac. Ewansiha was still pressed up behind him and Lukas could feel his cock hardening against his ass. His own responded.

Sergio smirked and turned around. He grabbed the pitcher and a stack of plastic cups then strutted towards the...back door?

"What—?"

"Hot tub!" he called over his shoulder. "It'll be good for King's...knee."

Chapter Nine

Left alone with Ewansiha, Lukas could feel the beginnings of uncertainty start to prod him, but he refused to succumb. He didn't want to lose the magical, erotic momentum they seemed to have found. It seemed like a dream and he didn't want to wake up.

He took two steps forward and began to undo the fastenings of his pants. He purposely didn't look back at Ewansiha, instead focusing on the French door that Sergio had disappeared out of. Before he shoved his pants down, he kicked off his loafers and bent slightly to hook a finger on each sock in turn, pulling them off.

Are you really going to do this?

Hell yes. Whatever came of tonight—whether a fun time to laugh with Sergio about later, an uncomfortable memory of awkwardness or the most erotic encounter of his life—Lukas wasn't about to call a halt and not experience it to the fullest.

He pushed his pants and briefs to his lower legs and stepped out of them. Only then did he turn around. And stare.

Lukas' jaw dropped at the bounty before him. Ewansiha had evidently not wasted any time getting over-dressed, making Lukas wonder whether he and Sergio had been in on this together. The only clothing in sight was a pair of what looked like black boxer briefs, in a heap on the floor beside King's large, bare feet. He traced his gaze up those familiar, muscular legs—the part of King's body he actually got to freely admire on a daily basis.

The upper thighs and above, though, was all new territory. Oh sure, he'd caught glimpses in the locker room, but never when he could look his fill.

And never when Ewansiha was erect.

Oh...my...God...

His cock was magnificent. Whereas Sergio's had hung downward because he was only partially erect, Ewansiha was fully hard, but hanging low owing to sheer weight, it seemed. Long, thick and corded with veins, dark as the rest of him, with the head even wider than the shaft, it made Lukas' mouth water to take his length as far as he could.

He couldn't tear his eyes away. "How the hell do you fit that thing in a jock?" he asked, only partially joking. Actually, not joking at all.

"Why don't we go join Sergio before he thinks we've ditched him?"

It struck Lukas that Ewansiha was hard without a woman in sight. That had to confirm that he was at least bisexual. Lukas finally blinked then took a good look at Ewansiha's narrow waist and the pronounced V-cut of his torso, up past the rippled muscles of his abdomen to his flat pecs and wide shoulders. Ewansiha tipped the corner of his mouth up in a smile that lit up his eyes.

"God in heaven," he muttered then forced himself to turn away and walk towards the door. His hand went—seemingly of its own volition—to his cock, which was hard as iron and aching for the touch. He stepped out and found himself on a large wraparound deck. Hearing the unmistakeable sound of bubbles around the corner to the left, he strode in that direction, releasing his cock. It bobbed with his steps and the cool night air heightened his awareness of his nudity.

He sensed Ewansiha following behind him and could almost feel the caress of his gaze zero in on his ass, which he knew had to seem blindingly white in the gloom, especially with the contrast to his tanned back and legs.

It was fairly dark on the deck even by the hot tub, but there was a glow from underwater and it illuminated Sergio, who was already seated, sipping his drink and watching them approach.

He stood and the water level reached just above his cock. Still, Lukas could see it just under the surface in the light. Sergio turned partially to the side where there was a tub-height counter along one side. He proceeded to pour two more drinks.

"Here you go." He held out the first to Lukas.

He climbed the steps to get in and accepted the cup before easing himself down.

Ewansiha joined them and Lukas thought he might decline the drink, but to his surprise he took the cup and held it up. "*Prost.*"

Lukas returned the toast and he took a sip. Yes, definitely a mojito, and a good one. He sipped some more then spread his arms out to rest them along the edges behind him. "Ahh…" The warmth seeped into him, lulling him into a relaxed state. He watched

Ewansiha, who was only a few feet away and whose calf was pressed against his. The blurred image of his cock was difficult to make out from this angle, especially with the jets going, so Lukas contented himself with gazing at those broad shoulders and intense eyes.

"You should get one of these," Sergio advised Lukas languidly. "Very good for after practices and games. And for when you have company over." He winked.

"Good mojitos, honey. Thank you," Ewansiha praised Sergio, who turned his sleepy smile to him.

"Why, you're very welcome." Sergio set down his cup then slowly glided through the water until he was straddling Ewansiha. He wrapped his arms around Ewansiha's neck and proceeded to pull him into a thorough, involved kiss.

When Ewansiha easily returned his embrace and tipped his head to deepen the kiss, it pretty much confirmed in Lukas' head that Ewansiha *was* bisexual or gay after all. Who knew?

Even with his reservations about King using Sergio for sex—since Serge was obviously a savvy, grown man capable of making his own decisions—the sight of the two of them together so close to him was an amazing aphrodisiac. His cock, which had softened since he'd got into the tub, began to perk up again as he watched Sergio and Ewansiha kiss. Without consciously willing it to happen, he too slid the very short distance across the hot tub until he was behind Sergio.

Ewansiha opened his eyes, though he didn't immediately release Sergio's lips. Their gazes met over Serge's shoulder, and Lukas was emboldened to press up against the trainer's back. A deep groan tore out of

Sergio when Lukas' hardening cock butted against his ass then slid along his crack.

A light touch to his arm caught his attention and he looked away from Ewansiha's eyes to see him tracing a random pattern on his skin with his fingers. It was as though Ewansiha wanted to touch him but wasn't sure how to initiate. Obviously he had a level of comfort with Sergio, but who knew how long it had taken them to achieve it? Of course, Sergio and Lukas had their own shared history, which was probably why he was in the middle...

His mouth opened as he suddenly realised what was happening.

You sneaky little matchmaker.

He thrust his hands around Serge's waist and pulled him back hard against him, muttering in his ear, "I know what you're up to."

Sergio laughed breathlessly. "It's about time one of you caught on. I swear, I was beginning to doubt my methods."

Ewansiha's eyebrows dipped slightly in confusion at their byplay, though he didn't relinquish his light hold on either of them.

"I'm going to trust that you know what you're doing and that it's not going to backfire and mess things up with the team." Lukas gave Sergio a light nip on his ear then stood. It felt good to get his torso out of the hot water. He was at a height where his cock rose just above water level but the cool air hitting it did little to douse the flames that were rising in him at the thought of being with the sexy Spaniard and the once-thought-unattainable Ewansiha.

"Don't worry, love. I know what I'm doing."

"Oh, don't I know it."

Sergio giggled and both Ewansiha and Lukas smiled in response. Lukas loved the sight of what he now thought of as King's 'real' smile. Sergio abruptly splashed to the side of the hot tub and climbed out. He walked around and bent over under the counter the drinks were sitting on, then emerged from underneath with a tote containing some rolled up towels, which he hefted up onto a bare spot on the counter.

"We're getting out?" Lukas asked, and looked at Ewansiha. A jolt of desire shot through him at the heated expression on his face. Sergio rejoined them in the hot tub.

"No way. Just making sure we're prepared for any eventuality." Sergio and Ewansiha exchanged a glance that seemed to indicate that they shared a secret. Curious, he moved over to take a closer look at the container.

He groaned as he found that, in addition to several towels, there were a couple of strips of condoms and a large tube of silicone lube.

"Handy," he managed as Sergio took him by the shoulders and turned him around.

"Up on the side." Sergio patted the edge of the tub behind him.

More than happy to let Sergio orchestrate the choreography, he hopped up where indicated and waited for what came next.

He didn't have long to wait, as Sergio gave him a sly look then bent to take his cock into his mouth.

"Oh, fuck," he gasped, leaning back a bit, wary of falling off. He managed to find a fairly secure position then surrendered to the feel of Sergio's expert mouth pulling his erection to even greater hardness than before.

Meanwhile, Ewansiha stood and reached into the bin then pulled out the lube. His cock was well on display above the water and Lukas couldn't look away. He uncapped the tube and squeezed some onto the fingers of his left hand.

"Hold him," Ewansiha instructed him, and when he used one arm to lift Sergio partially up so his ass was out of the water, Lukas figured out that he needed to support Sergio's upper body in order to keep the blow job going.

Sergio moaned, vibrating his cock with the sound, and Lukas looked up to see Ewansiha prepping Sergio by delving into his hole with the lube-slickened fingers. Lukas knew from experience that Sergio didn't need or want much stretching before sex…though with the girth of Ewansiha's cock, he might need more than usual.

His gaze bounced between Sergio's swollen lips around his cock, Ewansiha working Sergio's ass open and his hard-on skimming along the surface of the water.

After a while, Sergio pulled off him and groused breathlessly, "God, King, fuck me already."

Ewansiha didn't respond but withdrew his fingers, and Sergio turned around in Lukas' arms. This time Lukas didn't wait for instruction, but cradled Sergio with his back against Lukas' chest as they watched Ewansiha open and don a condom then add a layer of lube.

He approached them and his gaze locked on Lukas. Lukas had the sudden wish that he was the one Ewansiha was preparing to fuck with that intense look on his face.

Sergio gave a little hop upward and Lukas slid his hands under his thighs as Ewansiha positioned himself between his legs. He also reached under to support Sergio's ass with one hand and his touch brushed along Lukas' fingers.

Lukas' erection rubbed against Sergio's back and that tease of pressure was almost maddeningly light and inadequate. But this right now was more about Sergio, so he set his own desires aside. Leaning to the right, he could just reach the discarded tube of lube with his fingertips. He grabbed it and gathered some on his fingers before offering a squeeze to Ewansiha. Ewansiha applied that to Sergio's bared opening then proceeded to spread it around his hole with the tip of his cock.

Lukas reached with his lubed hand and grasped Sergio's cock just as Ewansiha eased into him.

"Ahh!" Sergio threw his head back against Lukas' chest as Lukas began to slowly jack him while Ewansiha gave a series of short thrusts and retreats until he had worked all the way into Sergio. He withdrew almost to the tip then surged forward, pushing Sergio against Lukas.

It was almost like he was fucking them both. Lukas ate up the sight of Ewansiha steadily fucking Sergio while Lukas worked his hard erection.

The timer for the jets shut off just then and the ensuing silence and calm made the sounds emanating from all three men that much sexier to Lukas' ears. It wasn't long before Sergio tensed in his arms and shot with a cry into the night air, cum covering his chest and Lukas' hand.

Ewansiha fucked him through it then slowly pulled out and discarded the condom over the side. He began stroking himself and Lukas couldn't wait any longer to get a hand on himself.

"Sorry, honey." He slid Sergio slightly to his left, enough so he could grab his own cock and work it. With his gaze locked on Ewansiha's erection sliding through his hand, he gave Serge's chest a swipe to gather his cum and used it for extra lubrication. Never had he been so hard before.

Then he was coming, head falling back and his eyes closing no matter how much he wanted to keep watching Ewansiha. He prised them back open just in time to see King jetting his own release all over Sergio's lower abdomen as he continued to float, sated, between them.

Their combined panting was all that could be heard for a few minutes after. Though he was hot as hell, he slid back down to sit in the water, wincing at the heat on his over-stimulated cock and balls. Sergio moved to sit close to him and Ewansiha dropped to the corner across from them.

"No, you get over here, mister." Sergio crooked his finger at Ewansiha, who smiled, then, with a great show of effort, moved across the tub to Sergio, who gave him a light kiss. Serge turned to kiss Lukas briefly then, in a sudden move that sent the water splashing, crossed to the other side of the tub and began to climb out.

When they simply watched him in surprise, Sergio rolled his eyes. He grabbed a towel and began to dry off. "My work here is done. Ice broken and all that. Where you go from here is up to you, but I personally would start with a yummy, slow post-coital kiss. Have fun, boys." With that, he winked and walked away into the dark towards the kitchen door, towel wrapped around his waist.

Lukas watched as he disappeared then swallowed and turned back towards Ewansiha. Instead of looking at where Sergio had gone, Ewansiha was watching him from mere inches away. No words were said as they moved slowly to bridge the short distance between them, hovering within breathing distance for a heartbeat before Lukas finally felt the first touch of Ewansiha's lips on his own.

His eyes drifted closed and they gradually, tentatively learnt the taste and feel of each other. Untold minutes passed as they kissed before Ewansiha pulled back.

"I'm hot. Are you?"

Yes, you are. And God yes... "Um, yes. About to pass out actually."

Ewansiha nodded. "Let's go in." The intimate sound of his deep voice did crazy things to Lukas' insides. He climbed out of the tub first, grabbed two towels then handed one to Ewansiha. He admired Ewansiha openly as he haphazardly dried off then tucked the towel around his waist. Only then did he realise that he was standing there naked and dripping and he hurried to catch up.

When they got back in the house, Lukas could tell from the unbroken silence that Sergio had left. *Well, hell. There goes my ride.*

He watched as Ewansiha locked the back door then faced him. "I guess Sergio left," Lukas pointed out unnecessarily.

Ewansiha walked to within a couple of feet of him then stopped. He reached out to touch his bare arm. "I can take you home."

"Okay." Lukas didn't know why, but he was a bit disappointed that the night would be coming to a close so quickly.

"Now? Or tomorrow morning?" Ewansiha asked, and a world of possibilities opened up for Lukas. Yes, it might really wreak havoc on their friendship and positions as teammates, and he really didn't know Ewansiha's story as far as being in closet went. But he really wanted to stay, to hell with the consequences. Of course, there was Xav to think of, but he supposed that as long as he let Xav know, he'd be okay there at home by himself till morning.

Ewansiha was watching him closely as though trying to ascertain the answer from Lukas' expression. He hadn't stopped stroking his arm.

He placed his own hand atop Ewansiha's and gave it a squeeze.

"After breakfast?" he offered, and Ewansiha grinned.

Chapter Ten

Ewansiha's alarm went off, and he tried to reach across the mattress to slap at the offending clock. Instead he found he couldn't move his arm, causing him to open his eyes. When he did, he found himself staring into the sleepy blue eyes of Lukas.

All the memories of what they'd done the night before rushed in. The fun they'd had with Sergio, then the mutual blow jobs they'd given each other after they'd gone up to Ewansiha's bedroom. After he'd come the second time, all his pills had worn off, and his knee had ached badly. He wouldn't have been able to get it up a third time, so they'd fallen asleep in each other's arms.

He licked his lips, unsure what to say to his teammate and the man who'd been starring in a few of his late night fantasies over the last couple of years. What exactly did he say when he'd managed to out himself in the most intimate way possible? It wasn't like he could go back and say, 'Sorry, the pain pills and alcohol made me do it'.

Hell, he wouldn't have done that anyway, even if it was the truth. Ewansiha had always tried to be honest, if only with himself. He wasn't going to hide being gay from Lukas by excusing it away. He knew the man wasn't going to out him, since it would be outing himself as well.

"Too much thinking going on for this early in the morning." Lukas' husky voice caused Ewansiha's cock to stiffen even more, which was saying something considering the impressive morning wood he'd woken up with.

Not wanting to listen to the thoughts and questions running around his head anymore, Ewansiha reached out with his free arm to cup the back of Lukas' head, then pulled the man towards him. Their lips met, and he tried not to think about how much he enjoyed kissing Lukas.

There was no way of knowing whether or not they were going to continue seeing each other or if it was just a one-off. No matter what Sergio thought, maybe Lukas wouldn't be interested in dating him, and if that was what ended up happening, then Ewansiha would bow out gracefully and deal with it.

He'd never truly enjoyed one-night stands, not deep inside. He'd always felt slightly dirty after engaging in one, but his career choice didn't make being out easy. So he'd been forced to hook up with guys in clubs or bars where they didn't recognise him, and he was never likely to run into them again.

Yet here he was kissing Lukas, whom he worked with every day. Things could go very wrong for both of them if they didn't decide how to handle it.

Lukas broke their kiss and scowled at him. "That's it, man. You're done thinking. I want you present in this bed when we fuck."

"I am." Ewansiha ducked his head when Lukas shot him a sceptical look. "Okay. Sorry. I'm turning my brain off."

"Good." Lukas shoved at his shoulder until Ewansiha rolled over onto his back.

Grasping Lukas' hips, he steadied him as Lukas straddled him. Lukas stretched to reach for the bottle of lube and a condom that had been tossed on the nightstand. Ewansiha ran his hands over Lukas' muscular chest and clearly defined abs.

"You don't know how hard it was to not stare at you when you walked around the locker room naked," he murmured. "I've never seen anyone as gorgeous as you."

"Not even Paolo?" Lukas grinned, then popped the top of the lube before he squirted some on his fingers.

Ewansiha snatched the slick away from his lover to put some on his fingers. He had a good idea what Lukas was about to do, and he wasn't going to let him have all the fun. Shaking his head, he answered Lukas' question. "I don't find Paolo attractive at all. Oh, I know he's probably one of the sexiest men in the world, but all I see when I look at him is a falling star. He'll blaze hot and fast for a little while, then plummet to the earth, burnt out and alone."

Lukas wrinkled his nose. "That's a depressing thought."

"Sorry. I've been around guys like him before, and none of them last long in the league. They burn too brightly." He slid his hand around to run his fingers along Lukas' crease, pausing only to rub them lightly over his hole. "We're going to take our time getting you ready."

"Hell yes, we are. It's going to take a lot of lube to get me ready for that beast you have between your legs."

Ewansiha blushed, still unable to get used to someone commenting on the size of his cock. It was a part of him, and he knew it was bigger than most, but so was the rest of him. He didn't say anything, just pressed the tip of his finger inside, stretching Lukas' ring of muscle.

Lukas' head dropped back as he moaned. "God, it's been a while since I've bottomed. I can't wait to get you inside me."

"Well then, help me out here," Ewansiha commanded, and Lukas joined him by shoving one of his own fingers deep inside his ass. Ewansiha rubbed his free hand over Lukas' chest. "Easy there, honey. Don't be in such a hurry. We still have lots of time before we have to be at the stadium for practice. I don't want you to hurt yourself."

Lukas met his concerned gaze with a bright smile. "Don't worry, King. I've finger-fucked myself lots of times. I know exactly how fast I can go."

"I guess I should trust you to know your own body," he muttered, deciding he should probably let Lukas set the pace.

They moved their hands together, each using one finger until Lukas nodded, signalling that he could take more. One became two, then two became three. That was when Ewansiha chose to take something else in hand, leaving the stretching to Lukas. After removing his fingers, he swiped his palm over the head of Lukas' cock, gathering the pre-cum that beaded there at his slit.

Using it along with some more lube, Ewansiha started jacking Lukas off. He pumped his hand in rhythm with Lukas thrusting his fingers into his opening. He watched as Lukas' eyes glazed over and desire welled up in them.

Finally, right when he was sure Lukas would come in his hand, Ewansiha was surprised when Lukas froze, one hand braced on Ewansiha's chest while he slowly eased the other out of his body.

"I want you to fuck me now, King. You don't know how long I've been thinking about this moment."

"Probably at least for as long as I have," he confessed as he searched through the sheets to find the foil packet. He tore it open. "Hands and knees, Lukas."

He grinned as Lukas scrambled to get in position, and he couldn't help but smack the pale cheeks that were presented to him.

"Hey." Lukas glared at him from over one shoulder. "None of that right now. One more and I'll come. I don't want to do that until you're filling me up."

"All right."

He rolled the rubber down his length, then squirted a generous amount of lube onto it. After coating it, he knelt between Lukas' legs, placing his cock at Lukas' opening. He took his time entering, pushing in an inch, then sliding back out. Each stroke in was a little farther. He knew, no matter how stretched and lubed Lukas was, he couldn't take all of Ewansiha's length at once.

Their groans filled the air when Ewansiha finally seated himself all the way inside Lukas. He ran his hand along Lukas' spine as he tried to relax him. He knew there had to be some burning, and he wasn't moving until Lukas told him it was okay. No matter how much his body protested.

"Are you okay?" He worried that he might have been too much for Lukas.

"Just give me another second," Lukas said, his voice strained like he spoke through clenched teeth.

Smoothing his hands over every inch of Lukas' body that he could reach, Ewansiha did his best to make his lover as comfortable as possible. He almost shouted when Lukas tilted his hips slightly, giving him the sign he'd been waiting for.

Ewansiha again started slowly, but his gentleness didn't last long as Lukas started moving with him, shoving back onto Ewansiha's erection each time he thrust in. Lukas fitted him like a glove, and the feel of the man's tight passage around him drove Ewansiha crazy.

He began slamming into Lukas, and Lukas begged him to go harder and faster. Well, Ewansiha could do that, and he did until sweat dripped down his chest to drop onto the small of Lukas' back.

When he glanced down to watch as he fucked Lukas, his climax tore through him like an explosion. He hadn't even realised how close he was until that moment. He flooded the condom with his cum, and held onto Lukas' hips so tightly he was sure he would bruise him. Yet he couldn't bring himself to worry.

After prising one hand away from Lukas, he reached around to encircle Lukas' cock. It only took two hard tugs to get Lukas to come as well. Moaning, Lukas dropped his head to his folded arms as he coated Ewansiha's hand.

They collapsed into a heap on the bed and Lukas squealed. Ewansiha had never thought he'd hear a guy make that sound. He barely managed to grab the base of the condom and make sure they didn't have a mess when Lukas rolled away from him.

"What the hell was that?" He pushed up on his hand to glance over at his lover.

"I hate being in the wet spot," Lukas groused.

Ewansiha started laughing, and couldn't stop. He sat up straighter, then gestured towards the bathroom. "Why don't we go take a shower, and get dressed? I can loan you some clothes to wear so you don't have to wear last night's."

Lukas nodded, then climbed out of bed. "Thanks. Hey, can I catch a ride back to my place before practice? I forgot I arranged to have my mechanic come check out a shimmy in my car while I was at the stadium."

"Sure. Good thing we don't live that far away from each other. Us showing up together might look odd if we did." Ewansiha padded into the other room, then took care of the condom. He turned on the water, letting it heat up.

"Yeah, you're right."

There was an odd tone in Lukas' voice, but before Ewansiha could ask him what was wrong, Ewansiha's phone rang. It was Silvia's ring, so he had to answer it.

"I have to answer this. Why don't you grab a shower? I'll take one at the stadium before practice."

He dashed over to snatch up his phone, then answered. "Hey there, darling."

"I need you to come with me to the doctor's today, Ewansiha. He said he can do the procedure and we'll know in a couple of weeks whether it worked or not." Silvia's excitement caused each word to rush and run into the other.

"I can't ask for another practice off, Sil. Our first match of the season is in three days. The coach is going to get pissed off if I'm not there." He pulled open one of his dresser drawers to rummage around for sweats and a T-shirt. He added socks to the pile.

Silvia sighed. "I know that, and I'd never get you in trouble with your coach. I talked to the doctor and he said that we could come in after your practice is done for the day. It doesn't matter to him how late, but it has to be today."

After pinching his phone between his ear and shoulder, Ewansiha grabbed a duffle bag out of his closet, then packed it with practice clothes. The shower had turned off, causing him to turn to watch as Lukas walked from the bathroom. He was speechless as he followed where Lukas' towel went, touching all the places Ewansiha discovered he wanted to lick.

Lukas looked up, and lust flared in the man's eyes for a moment. Ewansiha felt his cock trying valiantly to rise to the occasion again, but it just wasn't going to happen then.

"Ewansiha, are you still there?" Silvia asked, her impatience obvious in her voice.

"Yeah, love. I'm here."

Darkness filled Lukas' eyes, and he frowned. Ewansiha wondered what had happened in that brief moment of time while he talked to Silvia.

"So are you going to meet me at the doctor's office?"

"Why do I have to be there? Isn't this something you can do on your own?" He quickly tossed Lukas another pair of sweats and a T-shirt.

She huffed. "Yes, I can do it alone, but I don't want to. If Wendy can't be there with me, I'd like my best friend and soon-to-be father of my child there instead."

Her pleading tone got to him every time, and he grunted. "Fine. I'll meet you there after practice."

He held the phone away from his ear when she squealed so loudly he thought he would go deaf for a moment there.

"Thank you so much. I love you, Ewansiha Ajani Kroenig."

"I love you too, Sil. I'll text you when I'm done for the day."

After hanging up, he dressed, then shoved his feet into his tennis shoes. Lukas led the way out of the bedroom, and Ewansiha enjoyed the sight of Lukas' fine ass flexing in front of him as they climbed down the stairs.

Lukas declined when he asked if he wanted anything for breakfast, and Ewansiha again got the feeling that something was wrong, but he didn't have time to ask. If they didn't get going, they'd both be late for practice, and it could raise suspicions with the other guys.

After he pulled the car to a stop in front of Lukas' house, he leaned over to give him a kiss, but Lukas turned his head at the last moment, and Ewansiha's lips brushed his cheek.

"I'll see you at the stadium then," he said.

Lukas started to climb out of the car. "Yeah. Thanks."

"Oh shit!" Ewansiha slapped himself in the forehead. "I'm sorry, Lukas. If I didn't have to do this thing with Silvia, I'd give you a ride home as well, but it's really important to her and I promised yesterday I'd do it."

"That's cool, man. I understand. I'll get Sergio to bring me home today when we're done." Lukas gave him a slight wave before turning to walk away.

Yet the stiffness of Lukas' expression and shoulders told Ewansiha he didn't understand at all. There was no way Ewansiha could explain what was going on since it wasn't just his secret. He wasn't going to spill Silvia and Wendy's private life to a man he wasn't sure would be around in a personal way for more than a night or two.

"It shouldn't take us that long, though, so maybe I could stop by afterwards. I'll call you when we get done," he promised just before Lukas slammed the door shut.

He watched as Lukas stalked up to his front door, then disappeared behind it. Holy shit! Somehow he'd managed to screw up their relationship and they hadn't even been out on a date yet. That had to be some record for him.

Ewansiha put his car in gear before driving off. He was going to have to talk to Silvia about her crappy timing.

Oh my God, what the hell did I do? Lukas stomped through his house, feeling used, shaking his head at himself angrily. Truth be told, he wasn't sure exactly where his anger was directed. Himself for being a horny, hopeful fool. Sergio for instigating a hook-up with someone who was obviously, if not entirely, straight, at least publicly so. Or Ewansiha for being with him last night while he was involved with a woman.

'Sil', he'd said. Must be short for Silvia, that supermodel he had been seriously involved with a while back. Still was, from the conversation he'd overheard this morning, where *darling*s and *I love you*s had been tossed around with the casualness that only came from long use.

Lukas might be single and not opposed to casual hook-ups on occasion, and even though he didn't want Ewansiha to be a one-off, it was a little premature to ask for fidelity in return, but no way was he interested in being a secret fuck on the side. He had more pride than that.

"Everything okay?"

Xav's hesitant voice penetrated his mood and he forced himself to calm down and smile at the young man. After the first glance, his smile turned genuine. Far from the fragile boy he'd first met, Xav was looking healthier and more confident by the day. Dressed in a T-shirt and sweats, with his cell phone on the counter in front of him next to a crumb-laden dish and empty glass of milk, he could be any teenager having breakfast in any normal home.

Though... It wasn't a normal home. Lukas sighed. That's what he wanted for Xav, but was he the right person to give that to him? He shrugged off his doubts. He was all Xav had right now. The young man looking at him curiously didn't need him second-guessing himself, at least in that aspect. If he couldn't make good decisions about his love life, at least he could be a good surrogate dad-uncle-big brother for Xav.

"Yes, I'm fine. Just in a hurry to get to practice on time. How was last night?"

Xav gave him a wry smile. "Boring. How was it for you?" His smile turned sly.

"Not boring, and none of your business." He gave Xav a quelling look then looked at his plate. "What did you have for breakfast?"

"Streusel coffee cake."

Lukas searched his memory of what he might have had in the pantry. "We had coffee cake?"

Xav shrugged. "I made it after I looked up a recipe online. It was pretty easy." His cheeks coloured slightly.

A sharp burst of pride went through him. "Is there any left?" he asked, and Xav nodded.

He got up and went to the oven, then used a pad to pull out a small baking dish still more than half full of a crumbly-topped cake.

"Oh man, that looks good. Crap, I really have to run, though. Can I take some to go?"

"Yeah. Get your stuff or whatever and I'll put some in a napkin for you." Xav shooed him out of the kitchen.

Lukas hustled to get his bag put together then did a quick clean-up and brushed his teeth. He pelted down the stairs and skidded to a halt in the foyer. Xav was laughing at his haste, holding a to-go mug of something—hopefully coffee—in one hand and the promised napkin full of cake in the other.

He grinned back at Xav as he jammed his feet into his trainers, then pulled him in for a spontaneous hug, being careful of his full hands. When he let go, Xav still wore a smile, but his expression was thoughtful.

Lukas took his breakfast from Xav and made himself pause long enough to ask, "Okay?"

"Yeah. Everything's cool." He looked like he even believed it and Lukas counted that as a win. "You're coming back after practice?"

"Yes, definitely. Missed spending time with you last night." Lukas shifted impatiently, weighing his need to avoid being late with wanting to make sure Xav wasn't feeling ignored. "Maybe we can kick the ball around a little."

"Yeah?" Xav's face lit up. "That'd be cool." Xav brushed past him to open the front door. "Go on, don't be late. Dude," he added, looking exasperated when Lukas didn't immediately walk out. "I took care of myself just fine by myself before you came along."

"Hmm, well I don't know if 'fine' is the best word for it, but yeah, I know. You're not by yourself anymore, though, and you'd better get used to me checking on you. 'Kay?"

"Yeah, yeah." Xav's pleased smile belied his derisive dismissal.

Feeling much lighter than when he'd arrived, Lukas went to open his car then threw his bag on the passenger seat and climbed in. At Xav's frantic waving and gestures, he got back out to grab the breakfast items from where he'd put them on the roof. "Sheesh. Get your head on straight, Schulz," he muttered to himself.

Thankfully traffic wasn't too bad, and he got to the stadium in near record time. He parked where he'd told the mechanic he'd leave the car for his test drive and as arranged left the keys on top of the tyre under the wheel well, out of sight. He jogged towards the players' entrance, cursing as he noticed the time. Picking up the pace, he slammed the locker room door open and winced as a few of his teammates looked up in surprise.

"Jesus, make a little more noise next time. I think people the next town over are still asleep," Paolo complained with a wince. "Fuck, that hurt my head."

Lukas knew it was probably a hangover rather than his noise. "Sorry," he apologised anyway. He looked around surreptitiously while he opened his bag and his locker, but Ewansiha was nowhere in sight.

He quickly put on his socks, shin guards and cleats then hurried out of the door, glad that he wasn't the last one there when he got out to the practice area and found most of his teammates running to warm up. He eased into a small group and joined them, trying not to draw attention to himself.

Ewansiha wasn't out here either. Maybe in with Sergio? He shook his head, trying to stop thinking about the man and just concentrate on getting into the right headspace for practice.

After the group started breaking up, Lukas moved off by himself and started doing some of his footwork manoeuvres to kill some time until the practice began in earnest. He noticed Ewansiha and Paolo jogging out to the field together. After studying Ewansiha's form for any sign of his knee injury—it must be feeling decent today—he deliberately turned so that he was facing away from him.

Damned if he was going to give away any of his roiling emotions right now. He'd talk to Sergio after practice and find out what the hell the man had been thinking, getting him in this awkward situation.

Chapter Eleven

The practice went long as the coaches wanted to get some on-field real game situations run over and over, and Lukas could tell that Ewansiha was champing at the bit to get out of there.

And didn't that just rub him the wrong way.

Stop it, he told himself as he listened with half an ear to the shouted instructions from the coach. *No good can come of you getting moony over King... No matter how great last night was.*

Finally things wrapped up and Ewansiha all but sprinted to the locker room.

"Where you going so fast, King? Got a hot date?" Padraig yelled after him. It was hard to tell whether Ewansiha waved or flipped him off as he beat everyone to the building. "No woman's worth burning that much energy, trust me!"

Lukas bit his tongue as Padraig started in about how all of the women he'd dated had always kept him waiting, and that was why he rarely went back for 'second helpings'. *Ugh.*

He would've jogged ahead to get away, but he didn't exactly want to run into Ewansiha hurrying to meet Sil. So he tuned Padraig out the best he could and even fell back in the group a little bit. The showers would be full by the time he got in there, but he could kill some time.

Sergio. He could go see what the hell Serge had been up to when he'd instigated a hook-up between Lukas and King. Hell, they were close. He had to have known about his current involvement. He was a big boy and could make his own decisions, but Lukas found it hard to believe that Sergio would mess around with Ewansiha knowing he was a dirty secret on the side. Unless of course Serge had been deceived as well.

Lukas guessed that 'deceived' was a bit strong, considering that he hadn't even really thought about being together with Ewansiha until less than twenty-four hours ago. They certainly hadn't had a chance to talk it over and see where they each were coming from.

He found he'd walked on autopilot until he was outside Sergio's office, so he knocked and waited to be told to enter. After he got no response, he knocked again, then walked over to check the treatment room. No Sergio. *Damn.*

Rather than have it out with Sergio, Lukas ended up just grabbing his stuff and heading out to his car. Which was…gone. *Fuck.* For a moment, he panicked, then he remembered his mechanic. He pulled out his phone to check and, sure enough, there were a couple of missed calls and a voicemail message. Apparently the problem Lukas had noticed and had him come check out was something that needed immediate attention in the shop.

And my usual back-up ride I counted on when I set it up is off God knows where doing God knows what.

Lukas sighed and turned to walk back towards the building. He'd check one more time for Sergio then call a taxi or something. He pulled out his phone to start searching for a company, and was squinting at the screen when he noticed a shadow move in front of him.

"Hey, man, lost your car?"

Padraig's joke was actually pretty funny considering that he really had. Lukas gave a snort of laughter.

"Yes, actually." He made to walk past his teammate, still intent on his phone.

"Need a ride?" came the surprising offer.

Lukas stopped walking, staring at Padraig, considering it. He wasn't entirely sure whether he wanted to spend voluntary one-on-one time with him, but it would be a lot less hassle than waiting for a cab or trying to track down the suddenly elusive trainer. "You sure? I don't want you to go out of your way," he checked.

Padraig shrugged, looking uncomfortable in the role of Good Samaritan. "I don't have anything going on. And plus, now you'll owe me one." He smirked, looking more like the Padraig Lukas knew.

"Hey, asshole! Where are you going? You said you'd give me a ride!"

They both turned and watched Paolo scowling his way towards them.

"I haven't left yet, have I?" Padraig pointed out as Paolo caught up to them. Paolo gave his shoulder a shove. Padraig shoved him right back.

Oh brother. How did he get himself into these things? Lukas eyed his phone, debating about 'accidentally' calling a taxi after all.

"Come on. We're giving Lukas a lift too." Padraig strode off to his car, a sporty new silver Mercedes CLA four-door that he'd parked all by itself a distance away, probably to avoid door dings. Lukas couldn't blame him.

He looked around as they walked for Paolo's car, though he wasn't sure exactly what Paolo was driving these days. Some small, expensive convertible, knowing the goalie. He'd had at least three different cars that Lukas knew of since he'd joined the team. Plus, Paolo usually arrived later than Lukas. "Where's your car, Paolo?" he finally asked as they got into Padraig's car. He inhaled. God, that new car smell was amazing with the leather. Maybe he should think about getting a new car and giving the older model Audi to Xav...

Padraig burst out laughing, and Paolo smacked him on the back of his head from where he sat in the back seat. Lukas had been a bit surprised when Paolo had voluntarily headed to a rear door, leaving the passenger seat for him. "One of Paolo's women decided to drive herself home when she couldn't wake him up after they fucked, and she ended up ramming it into a sign pole."

"Was she hurt?" Lukas asked reflexively, turned sideways in the seat to look at Paolo.

He rolled his eyes. "She walked away without a scratch, but my Ferrari is going to need major repairs, if they decide they can fix it at all." He pouted slightly, shaking his head. "I loved that car."

"I tell ya, you have to put in a gate on your driveway. That way no one's going to steal your car."

"Idiot. If she had the car, she would've had the remote to the gate."

"Not if you did a numeric one," Padraig countered as they drove through the parking lot.

"Who wants to stop and punch in a number every time you leave the fucking house?"

Lukas sat back and tuned out their argument as best he could, enjoying the smooth ride. He purposely kept his mind clear of thoughts of Ewansiha. In fact, he did such a good job of not thinking of anything that it was only as they were approaching his neighbourhood that he realised that Padraig and Paolo might end up seeing Xav.

Fuck. He quickly pulled his phone out and prepared to text him, though saying what he wasn't sure. He didn't exactly want him to hide, but the idea of Xav being exposed to Padraig made him feel slightly ill.

"So what about your car, Lukas? I know you must've driven today because King got there way before you did. Spent fucking *hours* locked in with Sergio getting his *knee* worked on," Padraig exaggerated with a sneer.

Alarmed at the suggestive turn the conversation had taken, Lukas shut off his phone and quickly answered, "Yeah, had some kind of shimmy or vibration, and my mechanic took it in. What do you guys think it might be? Man, I hope it doesn't take too long to fix." He knew he was babbling, but he wanted to get Padraig off the topic of anything to do with innuendos about Sergio. He knew very well that Ewansiha would only have beaten him there by a max of thirty minutes, so he wasn't sure what Padraig's issue was.

Paolo thankfully chimed right in with his thoughts on what could be causing the problem with his car, displaying a somewhat surprising amount of knowledge about autos. Lukas had always thought of him as a talented but shallow partier—however his technical knowledge about high performance cars was well beyond anything Lukas could have mustered.

By the time they pulled into Lukas' drive, Paolo was ready to go commandeer his car from the mechanic and figure it out himself. "You come to me first from now on, hear me?"

"It's just an Audi, man," he soothed the animated goalie, smiling as he opened the door. His smile faded when Padraig turned off the engine and they both got out. Paolo tossed him his bag, which had been in the back seat next to him, and by then Padraig was already halfway to the front door.

He turned back to Lukas impatiently. "Well? Come on. I'm ready to get off my dogs and have a beer."

Before Lukas could figure out what to do, the decision was taken from him as the front door was thrown open. Xav stood in the doorway, mouth agape, barely flinching as the door rebounded and smacked him in the shoulder.

"Padraig O'Leary? Oh my God."

Padraig looked startled but soon recovered and smiled. "Hey, kid. What's your name?"

Xav shook his head, eyes wide with wonder. "Oh, um, Xav. Xavier, I guess but…"

"Hi, Xav. You a football fan?" Padraig was walking towards Xav. Lukas was frozen to the spot and could only watch as the two disappeared inside his house.

"Where'd he come from?" Paolo nudged him into motion and Lukas hurried towards the front door.

"He's staying with me for the time being."

Paolo started to ask another question but Lukas waved a hand to shush him and listened. Sounded like they were in the…kitchen? No. Garage? A door slammed and the murmur of voices and laughter began to get louder again.

"Seriously, Lukas, what's the deal with Xav?" Paolo broke the silence just as the other two came through from the kitchen into the empty dining room near the foyer, each holding a football in their hands.

Padraig stopped short and cocked his head. "Huh. Yeah. Obviously he's not your son, and you don't have a kid brother, right?"

Xav met Lukas' gaze and a bit of panic began to show in the worried crease between his eyes. He'd obviously been so overwhelmed at meeting his idol that it hadn't occurred to him that people might find his presence there strange. Lukas hadn't even thought beyond the day to day challenges to when he might need to explain Xav living with him. His mind raced as he tried for a plausible explanation.

"Not officially, no, but he's like a little brother to me. And he had some…uh…family issues, so I'm letting him live with me for a while."

"What kind of issues?"

"Okay, that's just rude, Paddy," Paolo thankfully interjected. "Why is it any business of yours what their personal shit is? So," he addressed himself to a quiet Xav, "do you play?" He took the ball from Xav's slackening grip as though not able to help himself. Probably couldn't.

"Well, I used to," Xav answered hesitantly. "Just for school. I mean, I'm not that good or anything. Not like you guys." A bit of his initial excitement began to return to replace the uncertainty on his face. "I can't believe I'm getting to meet you guys. In person!"

Padraig's eyes were still narrowed with curiosity, but he predictably let the fan worship stroke his ego. "Well, I'm super glad to meet you too. You want to kick it around a bit while our host gets something organised for food?"

Xav's eyes went wide and he looked at Lukas hopefully.

Thankful that the uncomfortable line of questioning seemed to have been diverted, at least for the time being, Lukas resorted to his usual comeback for his house-crashing teammates. "Why the hell do I have to feed you guys? What am I—your mother?"

"I can make something," Xav offered even as he looked wistfully towards the living room and the back door beyond.

"Nah, go ahead and have fun. I'll just put out some old leftover junk and snacks like I *always* do for these *ungrateful hooligans*." He raised his voice to make sure the targets heard him.

Padraig and Paolo laughed as he'd intended and walked through the living room then out of the door to the backyard. At an encouraging gesture from Lukas, Xav grinned and ran to join them.

"How'd you end up with those two here today? Season hasn't even started yet."

Lukas spun around towards the front door at the sound of Sergio's voice. "Where the fuck were you today? I so have a bone to pick with you!"

Sergio raised his eyebrows and hands in mock surrender.

"But I can't *now*," Lukas continued, gesturing at the backyard. The sounds of the three of them passing the football came in through the door. Normally Xav's excited voice mixing in with the deeper voices of his idols would have brought a smile to his face. He started to pace, unable to stand still any longer, what with the stress of having Padraig and Xav in the same place, not knowing what to do about Ewansiha and his worry and anger about Ewansiha's duplicitous relationships, having sex with Silvia and him and Sergio…

God, was there anyone *else* he didn't know about? He threw his hands up in frustration and headed through the dining room to the kitchen, Sergio on his heels.

"You need to simmer down, love. You're going to burst something."

Lukas just glared at Sergio as he began to pull chips and crackers and bread out of the pantry. Sergio shrugged then moved to the fridge, opened it and stood staring inside.

Lukas snorted and shoved him out of the way before he began to retrieve what he'd need for dips and sandwich makings. "Here." He thrust a couple of bags of prepared vegetables into his hands. "Make yourself useful, at least, and start putting those on a platter."

Sergio moved towards the cupboard he kept his plates in. "No problem."

At the agreeable words, Lukas' temper boiled over. "No problem? Is that all you have to say?" He straightened and shut the fridge, then lowered his voice to a harsh whisper, conscious that at any moment someone could come back inside. "You hooked me up with King—don't you tell me you didn't plan it—and you had to know that he's in a serious relationship with a woman. For that matter, you need to have more self-respect than to mess around with a guy that far in the closet. What the hell?" He made himself stop talking and began to ferociously rip open packages of cheese and sliced meat.

"Ouch. Take it easy on the meat." Sergio stopped arranging the vegetables and put his hands over Lukas', stilling them on the counter.

"Am I interrupting something?"

They both whipped around to find Ewansiha grinning at them from the dining room doorway, dressed in running clothes. "I knocked but no one heard me. Door was open." His smile faltered when his gaze met Lukas'. "Is something wrong? And is that Padraig's new car out front?" He sobered completely, looking around as though searching for signs of their teammate before looking back at Lukas. "What's going on?"

"Nothing. What brings you by?" Lukas hated the way the terse, unwelcoming response sounded coming out of his mouth.

Ewansiha looked taken aback by the question and a bit uncomfortable. "I was just out for a walk, loosening up my knee. Saw the cars and I knew at least Sergio was here, though I wasn't sure about the other…" He trailed off. "Are you okay?" His gaze flicked to Sergio then back again. He lowered his voice. "You look upset. Is it about…what happened?"

His eyes went immediately back to Sergio and widened. Lukas glanced over in time to see Sergio making a slashing motion across his neck that he abruptly turned into a scratch behind his ear. "Sooo, are you thinking build-their-own sandwiches or should we just make a bunch up? Here, Padraig"—he took the lid off some dip and unceremoniously plunked it in the middle of the vegetables—"take this outside."

Lukas turned to see Padraig at the living room entrance.

"Vegetables? Seriously?" Padraig came in, frowning at Sergio. "When did you get here? I didn't know you were coming."

"Xav's a growing boy, and it wouldn't hurt you to eat more healthily either, especially now that the season's going to be starting. And I got here a few minutes ago, just before Ewansiha."

Padraig gave a dramatic startled impression that Lukas had a feeling wasn't entirely faked as he whipped his head to the side to look at his teammate in the other doorway. "King? What the hell are *you* doing here?"

Ewansiha shrugged. "You know I live nearby. Saw the cars so just popped in. How about you?"

"Oh, we gave Lukas a ride home…since you ditched him. Which is fine since we were overdue for a night over, eating him out of house and home. He misses us and gets lonely if we don't stop by at least once a week during the season." Padraig made obnoxious kissy noises at Lukas.

"We?" was all Ewansiha asked. Lukas figured he had just expected to see Sergio and him…well, and Xav. It occurred to him that King hadn't really met the young man yet, other than the day he'd dropped by and had first seen him. It would be nice for them to get to know each other…

Lukas shook his head, immediately irritated with himself for caring whether Ewansiha and Xav got along.

"Yeah, me and Paolo. He's in the backyard with the kid… What's his name? Xav, right?" Padraig spun back towards Ewansiha. "That's right! Speaking of kids, I heard you're going to be a daddy soon." He shook his head mournfully.

Lukas reeled in shock. "What?" This was said simultaneously by Ewansiha, Sergio and Lukas as everyone turned to face King. Lukas waited for Ewansiha to laugh…but he didn't. All Lukas could read on Ewansiha's face was surprise and embarrassment and…guilt? "Where did you hear that?" King asked quietly.

"Hey! Paolo!" Padraig hollered out of the kitchen window. The regular, familiar thudding of a football being passed ceased.

"What?" came the yell back.

"What paper was that in, about King having a baby?" Lukas watched as King winced.

A pause. "Fuck if I remember. A couple of the gossip rags. Why?"

"He's here!"

"Who's here?"

"King!"

"King's here? Really?"

"Jesus, would you quit fucking yelling out my window? My neighbours are going to freak," Lukas grumbled, desperate to stop this conversation. Sergio was staring at Ewansiha, who was looking intently at the floor.

Footsteps sounded in the living room then Paolo came skidding around the corner of the kitchen entry. Xav followed at a slower pace.

"King! Congrats, man. Gonna be a daddy? Do you know for sure yet?"

"I don't know what you guys are talking about."

But he *did*—that much Lukas could tell, and his stomach churned as his fanciful hopes plummeted.

"*Sure* you don't," Padraig chimed in. "That's why there's a picture in the papers of you hugging that hot model Silvia after coming out of one of the most exclusive obstetrics and fertility clinics in the country. And someone in the doctor's office anonymously confirmed that you two are trying to have a kid. So, did you knock her up?" He grinned. "Your boys working down there?"

Lukas exchanged uncomfortable glances with Sergio then Xav, who edged a bit closer to Serge. "Cut him some slack. What are you, the paparazzi?" Sergio finally joined in the conversation. "I'm not surprised Padraig's being an ass about it, but I expected better from you, Paolo."

"Hey!" Padraig responded. "I'm not an ass. Though mine *is* fine."

"Well, hell, we're his friends—his mates. I figured the photos looked pretty legit and I was just trying to be supportive," Paolo defended himself. "Whatever. Not that big a thing, having a *baby*." He widened his eyes sarcastically then rolled them. "Anyway, sandwiches, huh? What, no mustard? Xav, can you check for some in the fridge?"

Lukas stood mute in the midst of the chaos in his kitchen, while Ewansiha did the same near the doorway. Every time Lukas glanced at him, King was looking away from him. Sergio and Paolo orchestrated the group into a buffet line and they fixed plates of food then one by one carried them outside until Serge walked to the doorway with his plate. He turned and gave Lukas a sympathetic glance then gestured at King, mimed talking and left them alone.

Nice try, but not sure if talking is something we can actually do.

Chapter Twelve

Silence reigned in the kitchen in the wake of Sergio's departure. Lukas waited for a few moments until he heard the sound of his back door closing, then he glanced warily at the open window Padraig and Paolo had been yelling through.

"Come on." He beckoned Ewansiha to follow him. Without seeing whether he was complying, he led the way out of the kitchen and upstairs before he paused. He didn't really want to talk in his bedroom, but he didn't want to invade Xav's privacy and use that room, either.

Sighing, he walked into his room and waited for Ewansiha to enter, then shut the door. After a moment's consideration, he locked it then joined Ewansiha where he was standing in the dead centre of the room.

The bed seemed to loom large as they waited in silence for the other one to speak. Now that they were alone, having known every inch of Ewansiha's body, he experienced an awareness he'd never known before—as though every minute movement and expression Ewansiha made, every breath, was seized by his brain and analysed.

Lukas sighed without being aware that he was going to do so. That, at least, seemed to break the impasse and Ewansiha finally cleared his throat.

"I'm sorry. That wasn't how I wanted you to find out."

Well, that sounded like a death knell for anything being possible between them. Lukas made himself meet Ewansiha's gaze now that the big man was finally looking at him. He processed his statement, feeling a bit numb.

"Find out..." he prompted hoarsely, though he wasn't sure he wanted to know.

Here we go. Here's where he tells me he's really with her...but he wants to still see me on the side...

"Silvia asked me to donate sperm so she can have a baby."

He immediately noted the pronoun. *She. Not we.* Knowing full well he shouldn't be relieved by what might have been a slip of the tongue, he nevertheless repeated it, trying not to look as hopeful as he felt. "She?"

Ewansiha's eyes shifted to the side, but he nodded. "Yes, she. We're just friends now."

Lukas wondered about the hint of evasion he sensed, but finally put it down to nervousness. He'd never known Ewansiha to lie to him. "So she's...using your sperm to make a baby that she's going to raise on her own," he clarified.

His scepticism must've been clear on his face because Ewansiha frowned slightly and took a step forward to cup Lukas' elbow lightly. "I'll still be the father, but we're not going to get married, be a couple or even live together. I..." He paused and swallowed hard. "I don't know if I'm ready to be a father. I don't know how."

The surprising crack in Ewansiha's customary control tugged at Lukas and he in turn reached out to run his hands along Ewansiha's arms to reassure him. "You'll be a great father, I know. Don't worry. No one starts off knowing what to do. You'll learn along the way, but you're a good person, so I know that will translate over to parenthood as well."

Ewansiha sighed and shrugged, but Lukas noticed he didn't move away from his touch. If anything, he leaned in. "I suppose. It's just all happened so fast." He looked directly at Lukas and Lukas felt his stare all the way down to his toes. "Kind of like us."

Lukas parted his lips and dropped his gaze to Ewansiha's mouth. "How fast could we have happened? We've been teammates for years."

"Yes, but I didn't realise we were playing on the same team."

He knew King wasn't talking about football anymore. "You had to suspect, knowing that Serge and I were friends."

"Suspect? Maybe a little. Hoped? Yeah. But I didn't want to take a chance on messing things up." A worried frown puckered Ewansiha's brow and he shifted restlessly. "I hated how it was at practice today. That was my worst fear come true."

"For me too," Lukas admitted. "I really had no idea you liked men at all. You come across straight as a ruler."

"So you thought I was straight, but... You were interested anyway?"

"Now you're just fishing." Lukas mock glared at him, enjoying the close banter. He was uber-aware of his bed right behind him. A daring part of him wondered if they had time for a quickie before they rejoined the group.

Ewansiha just raised an eyebrow at him.

"Fine," he muttered. "I thought you were hot and had a man-crush on you. Happy?"

"Very." With that Ewansiha ended the discussion and sealed their reconciliation with a breath-stealing kiss. Lukas plastered himself up against Ewansiha's taller form, loving the way they fitted together, loving the way he suddenly had free access to the man he'd been lusting after for ages.

Aware that time was ticking away with people just out in the yard, he made a snap decision and dropped to his knees. Ewansiha was in running shorts and he discovered when he tried to yank them down that they'd been tied at the waist. He scrambled to undo the string.

"Lukas…"

"Shh." He didn't want to get in a discussion, he just wanted the gorgeous black cock he felt increasing in size beneath his hand in his mouth as soon as possible.

He finally got the damn knot undone and slid the shorts down enough to bare Ewansiha's growing erection. Without hesitation, he took it in his mouth. A tang of salt from sweat combined with a burst of bitter pre-cum as he used his hand to jack the base while working the tip with his mouth. He glanced up from under his lashes, and the rapt expression on Ewansiha's face stole what breath he had left.

Ewansiha looked frozen in the act of reaching for Lukas, his hand hovered just to the side of his head. Lukas grabbed it and placed it on his head in a wordless command for him to take a more active role. A groan rolled up from deep inside Ewansiha and he ran his hand over Lukas' short hair before cupping the back of his head.

He gave an experimental thrust that Lukas welcomed, while using his fist low on Ewansiha's cock to control the depth of his penetration. They finally worked out a rhythm that enabled Lukas reaching to free his own aching shaft from his shorts so he could stroke it in time with Ewansiha's movements.

"Lukas, Lukas…" Ewansiha softly groaned then began fucking his mouth in earnest. Lukas increased his suction and the motion of his hands, so close himself, but wanting to get Ewansiha off first.

"Lukas!"

That wasn't King. Breathing hard, Lukas tore his mouth away from Ewansiha's cock as his name was called from somewhere in the house, a little too close by for comfort.

"Yeah?" he responded hoarsely. He wasn't even sure who was looking for him, not having recognised the voice through his fog of arousal.

"We want to play some ball and everyone's almost done eating. Are you guys coming?" He thought it might be Paolo.

Ewansiha muttered, "Almost," and pressed Lukas back towards his groin. Lukas stifled a laugh.

"Be right there!" He hoped his voice sounded steadier and less fucked-out than he felt. He gave Ewansiha's cock his full attention, sucking him into his mouth and working him while he handled his own erection roughly, doing what he needed to get them both there.

"Be careful with that beautiful cock. I want to have some fun with that later. Oh God." Ewansiha was breathing hard then he stopped altogether as he shot cum against the back of Lukas' throat. Lukas pulled backward a little to catch the next spurt on his cupped tongue, looking up at this teammate as he did so. Ewansiha groaned again and Lukas jacked him lightly, milking him of the last bits of cum onto his palm then using it on his own straining cock to smooth the glide of his hand.

It didn't take more than a dozen or so strokes before he was shooting into his hand as Ewansiha petted his head, using his fingers to trace random patterns on his hair and face. He sat back on his heels, trying to get his breathing under control, then grimaced at the handful of cum. He glanced around and saw the T-shirt Ewansiha had lent him that morning lying on a chair. He knee-walked over to it and made a show of wiping his hand.

Ewansiha fought a smile as he adjusted his shorts. "Oh sure. Use my shirt. I was going to tell you to bring it back tonight, but..."

"Yeah?" A glow of happiness went through Lukas. He stood and fixed his own shorts then walked into Ewansiha's welcoming arms. "You want me to come over tonight?" He allowed himself a few moments of affection before he reluctantly parted from Ewansiha and walked to the door.

"Definitely, if that's what you want."

Lukas smiled. "I want."

* * * *

Ewansiha had left Lukas' house an hour ago, not wanting to look like he was waiting around for the rest to leave. He'd forgotten that some guys on the team liked to hang out at Lukas'. He should've checked before showing up like that, but he'd been so eager to see Lukas after being away from him for most of the afternoon.

Silvia had told him he could tell Lukas the truth about the baby and her and Wendy. Yet he hadn't felt comfortable exposing the women's relationship to Lukas, not that Ewansiha thought Lukas would react badly to it. It was just that he hated when his own privacy was compromised, and he wanted to protect Silvia and Wendy for as long as he could.

When the doorbell rang, Ewansiha walked from the game room he had at the back of the house to answer it. Smiling, he opened it to find Lukas standing on his front steps, holding a duffle bag. He grabbed Lukas' hand, then jerked him inside.

"Glad to see you missed me," Lukas teased and Ewansiha wrapped his arms around his waist.

After squatting slightly, he put his shoulder into Lukas' stomach, then lifted.

"What the fuck? Dude, you shouldn't be doing that. I'm not exactly light."

"Just hold onto your bag, and I'll worry about getting us where we need to go." He wasn't going to take Lukas upstairs because he knew his knee wouldn't stand for that. But he could get him to the couch in the game room, and that was a good spot for some loving.

It was close to the hot tub as well, where he planned on doing some soaking later on. Not at the moment, though. He ran his hand over one of the firm globes of Lukas' ass, then squeezed one. Lukas squirmed, and Ewansiha smacked him.

"Don't wiggle or I'll drop you on your head. That would be a little difficult to explain to the doctors."

Lukas froze, giving him the opportunity to get them both to the room without any injuries to either of them. He set Lukas down next to the couch, then shoved him so he tipped over onto the cushions.

He couldn't drop to his knees in the dramatic motion that Lukas had earlier, but he could get to the floor. Lukas must have read his mind because by the time Ewansiha was on his knees between Lukas' thighs, Lukas had his pants open and was stroking his cock.

"That's mine," Ewansiha told him as he swatted Lukas' hand out of the way.

But before he put his mouth on it, he stripped Lukas' pants and underwear the rest of the way off. Once Lukas was naked, Ewansiha focused on the thick cock in front of his face. It wasn't as long or as big around as his, but it was still impressive.

Leaning forward, he pressed his lips in a soft kiss to the spongy head of Lukas' shaft. Then he licked the pre-cum where it leaked from the slit. He wrinkled his nose at the bitter taste, remembering why he rarely gave head. Yet he wanted to taste him and feel what it was like to have Lukas in his mouth.

Ewansiha lifted his gaze to meet Lukas', and his cheeks warmed at the emotion he saw in Lukas' eyes. No one had ever looked at him like he was the centre of their world, not even any of the women he'd dated. He trailed his fingers along the crease near Lukas' hip. He loved how Lukas shuddered at his touch.

Breathing deeply, he slid his lips down Lukas' length to brush his nose against the pubic hair at its base. He swallowed, then began to bob his head up and down. Lukas cradled the back of his head, but his touch wasn't anything more than gentle encouragement.

"Jesus, your mouth is amazing," Lukas said, then moaned as Ewansiha deep-throated him again.

He tugged on Lukas' legs, pulling him closer to the edge of the couch so he could run one of his fingers around Lukas' puckered opening. Lukas planted his feet on the floor to arch his hips up off the cushion, obviously wanting more of Ewansiha's touch.

Letting Lukas' cock slip from his mouth, he rocked back on his heels and tapped his lover on the knee. "There's a bottle of lube and a condom on the table right behind your head," he told him.

He enjoyed the sight of Lukas stretching his arm behind him to find the supplies. While he waited, Ewansiha continued to jerk Lukas off, using his spit to ease the friction slightly. When Lukas grunted to let him know he'd got the stuff, Ewansiha held up his fingers for the man to coat them with lube.

That done, he took all of Lukas' length in again while teasing and playing with his hole. At just the right moment, when he'd taken Lukas in as far as he could, he breached it with his fingers.

"Fuck!" Lukas shouted, his body bowed as Ewansiha did his best to overwhelm him with pleasure.

Ewansiha didn't let up either, allowing Lukas to fuck his face while he impaled himself on Ewansiha's fingers. He bent them enough to nail Lukas' gland, knowing it was driving him crazy.

Lukas' cock swelled in his mouth, causing Ewansiha to gag slightly. He let Lukas ease out until only his head remained. He pressed the tip of his tongue into the slit, and Lukas jerked. His pre-cum covered Ewansiha's mouth, and he knew Lukas was close.

He pulled away, and Lukas whimpered, a hint of protest in that sound. He grabbed Lukas' hand then encircled Lukas' cock with it.

"Don't come yet. I want to be in you when you do."

He climbed to his feet then practically tore his clothes off to get naked. After spotting the condom Lukas had dropped on the couch next to him, Ewansiha grabbed it. He ripped it open, managing to get it on without tearing it despite the fact that his hands were shaking so badly.

Once he was covered and the rubber slicked up, he positioned himself at Lukas' hole, then as he stared into Lukas' blue eyes, he slowly pushed in. He filled his lover's ass until he couldn't anymore.

Ewansiha froze, his hands resting on Lukas' hips. "Are you okay?"

Lukas bit his bottom lip as he seemed to think about it, then he nodded. "I'm fine."

"Good."

He started pumping in and out of Lukas, hard and fast. He wished he could take it slow, but everything inside him wanted to claim Lukas in the most primal way possible. It was totally different from any of his other relationships. Before, he'd never cared whether they stuck around or not. Well, except for Silvia.

Yet Ewansiha suddenly couldn't imagine his life without Lukas, and while the new thought scared him, it rushed through him with such power that he came, spilling his cum into the condom.

Lukas moaned, and Ewansiha realised he hadn't come yet. After bracing his body on one hand, Ewansiha covered Lukas' fingers with his own. His tight grip forced Lukas to move as well, and when Lukas came, his inner muscles massaged some more out of Ewansiha's cock.

Cum blanketed their hands, and Ewansiha knew he had to clean them up before his knees gave out on him. Gritting his teeth, he pushed to his feet, keeping his clean hand around the base of the condom so as not to lose it.

After taking care of everything in the kitchen, plus cleaning up, he brought a cloth back to where Lukas was sprawled on the couch. He washed his lover's body, then stood back up. He held out his hand to Lukas.

"Let's go to bed. We have our first game tomorrow, and we both need our sleep."

Lukas let him pull him upright, then moved right into Ewansiha's embrace. He held Lukas close for a few seconds, absorbing his warmth and the honest smell of sweat and sex. He nuzzled Lukas' temple in affection.

He heard Lukas mumble something, and could tell he was dead on his feet. Smiling, Ewansiha escorted Lukas through the first floor, turning off lights as they went. He set the security system, then helped Lukas upstairs.

Once in his room, he tucked Lukas in then crawled in next to him. Ewansiha set his alarm so he didn't oversleep. He liked getting up early on game days, and it would help him get into the right mental place. This game would be hard, especially after coming back from injury.

"Good night, Lukas." He brushed a kiss over Lukas' cheek, then pulled him close.

"Sweet dreams, King," Lukas murmured, already falling asleep. "I love sleeping with you."

Ewansiha didn't have to think about his response. "I love sharing my bed with you. Maybe someday it can be our bed," he whispered.

Chapter Thirteen

The stadium vibrated with the stomping and chanting of the fans as the teams came out onto the field. Ewansiha felt the energy rise from the soles of his cleats up through his legs into his chest. It was almost like being at a rock concert and feeling the bass drive the beat of his heart until he thought it would come out of his chest.

His cock stiffened, and he was happy his shorts were baggy enough that none of his fellow teammates would notice. Of course, he was pretty sure most of them sported hard-ons of their own. The excitement of the fans and the adrenaline of the players conspired to get them all hornier than monkeys.

Lukas jogged down the sideline next to him, and Ewansiha did his best not to stare at him. Waking up to find him in his bed that morning had freaked Ewansiha out a little. What had freaked him out was how right it felt to have the blond in his arms and sharing his bed.

"Heads up, King."

He looked up in time to catch the ball Padraig had thrown at him. *Guess I should be happy he warned me instead of just letting it hit me in the face.* Allowing the ball to drop to the ground, he began kicking it from foot to foot as he ran along.

"Hey, Schulz," he called, and when Lukas glanced over at him, he kicked the ball to him. Lukas took it in his stride, then proceeded to return it to him without pausing.

They ran some more warm-up drills, including Paolo and Padraig along with the other guys who were going to be starting the match. Ewansiha would start, but he knew that later in the second half, when it got close to the referee calling time, the coach would pull him to put Lukas in. He was fine with that because his knee would be screaming by that time, and he'd be ready to call it quits for the day.

Their last practice had been run at full speed, and he'd needed Sergio's magic hands and a tub full of ice to be able to walk out on his own two feet yesterday. His doctors had all promised him that the ache would fade over time, but Ewansiha was afraid that there would always be some lingering pain, waiting to take him out at the most inopportune times. He wanted to be able to play football for several more years, but he wasn't positive that was going to happen.

He and the other nine men who would be starting the first match of the new season lined up to take shots at Paolo in goal. The man clapped his yellow gloves together, jeering at them, arrogant as always about being able to keep the ball out of the net.

Ewansiha knew how to score on Paolo, having played on the same team with him for five years and having studied the man's every move. He'd offered to show Paolo what the goalkeeper was doing to telegraph his moves, but so far Paolo hadn't taken him up on it.

He jogged slowly towards Paolo, keeping his gaze on the man, not the ball at his feet. He'd always had a sixth sense about where the ball was at all times, whether he had it or someone else did. Ewansiha watched Paolo, waiting for the right moment. *There!*

Paolo had shifted his weight to his left foot, putting all of it on his heel like he thought Ewansiha would kick the ball to the right, and Paolo would have to push off with that foot. It would put him off balance, not giving him enough time to react to Ewansiha's kick.

Ewansiha drove his foot forward, propelling the ball as fast as he could towards Paolo. The goalie reacted too late, and the ball hit the back of the net. Paolo glared at him, but Ewansiha simply nodded to the man before taking off back to the team's bench. He didn't need to take any more shots to prove that he had Paolo's number.

"You always score on him, even during mock games," Lukas said softly under his breath as they took sips of Gatorade while waiting for the coach to give them last minute advice.

He shrugged. "It's not hard when you know what to look for, though I try not to score too often because I don't want Paolo to know I figured out his tells. I've tried telling him, but he hasn't listened to me yet."

Lukas shot him a quick look. "Will you show me?"

"Tonight at my place, we'll go over some game footage, and I'll point out what I'm looking for before I hit the ball at Paolo."

"Thanks." Lukas bumped their shoulders together, just like two normal teammates would before a game.

"No problem, man. You're going to be taking my place at some point. Want to make sure you're as good as you can be before that happens." Ewansiha had never been against sharing his secrets with teammates he liked—he'd never understood men who didn't try to help the people they worked with. When one of them got better at his position, all of them got better as a team.

"All right, men. You know the game strategy. Kroenig, I want you playing centre back to start. Defending might be easier on your knee. We'll get you back playing centre forward by the third match."

Nodding, Ewansiha wasn't going to complain. Part of his usefulness on the team was the fact that he could play both forward and defender positions, though he was stronger as a centre forward. Yet the coach knew best, and he still wasn't at a hundred per cent, no matter what the doctors had told him.

"Time to go, gentlemen," the referee told them as he ran past to the centre of the pitch.

"O'Leary, you're centre forward this match. The rest of you know where your spots are." The coach gestured for Padraig to go to the middle of the pitch to do the coin flip.

Their team lost the toss, but none of them were worried about it. Once their opponents chose which goal they wanted to attack, everyone took their positions. Ewansiha settled in his spot, then shot Lukas a quick glance.

Lukas grinned at him before giving him a wink. Chuckling, Ewansiha shook his head slightly before slipping into his game mentality. The pitch wasn't the place for him to get distracted by his lover.

When he played football, Ewansiha never paid attention to the fans in the stands or the teams on the sides of the pitch. All he focused on was the ball and the feet that were passing it from body to body. Instinctively he knew which player had the ball, where they were going with it and exactly where his body needed to be to intercept it.

On the field and in the middle of a match, there was no outside world to bother him. He didn't have to worry about what the media was saying about Silvia being pregnant or whether he was the father or not. All he had to worry about was doing his job, which was to keep the other team from scoring.

"King!" Padraig shouted to him, and he waved his hand, letting the captain know he saw the approaching player.

The attacking centre forward was the opposite team's best player, and he'd outpaced the rest of Ewansiha's team. So it was Ewansiha's job to ensure that the ball didn't reach Paolo. As talented as Paolo was, he couldn't stop every goal, and Ewansiha needed to help him out.

The centre tensed his leg, alerting Ewansiha that he was about to kick. Shooting across the pitch, he launched his body into the air, heading the ball back towards where Padraig stood. When he landed, he shook his head and shoulders, loosening the tension from the impact.

As the match progressed, he and his fellow defenders stopped more balls, but a few got through and Paolo showed why he was considered one of the best goalies in the league. Unfortunately, right before the referee stopped the match for half-time, the other team broke free and their best striker managed to get one by Paolo.

The goalie was pissed off as they jogged into the locker room. Ewansiha limped to where his locker was, trying hard not to wince each time he put his foot down on the floor. Sergio was waiting for him, and he pointed to the bench. After Ewansiha sat, Sergio wrapped his knee in ice.

"I can't believe he shot it by me. I thought I had it stopped." Paolo slammed his locker door shut, then dropped to the bench as he pouted.

"We're only down a goal, Paolo. We can make that up next half." Padraig patted Paolo's shoulder as he walked past him.

"Does anyone have any idea how many penalty minutes we'll be playing yet?" one of the other mid-fielders asked.

No one said anything because no one ever could be entirely sure how much longer beyond the regulation ninety minutes the match would go. Leaning back against his locker, Ewansiha closed his eyes, trying to relax and deal with the pain in his knee.

Apparently all the full speed practices hadn't been fast enough to get his knee ready for the match. He didn't know if he was going to be able to play the next half. Lukas sat next to him.

"Are you all right?"

Ewansiha shrugged. "I'm not sure. My knee isn't doing too hot. Not sure if it's going to hold up to the rest of the game."

"Do you want Sergio to come over and check it out again?" Lukas asked, even though he was already waving at Sergio where the man stood near Padraig.

Sergio grabbed his bag, then joined them. He crouched next to Ewansiha, flexing his knee and checking for range of motion. Ewansiha winced as it reached a certain point, and Sergio noticed.

"I'm going to tell the coach that I can't finish the game." Ewansiha looked over at Lukas. "You'll get to play earlier in the match than we thought."

"I can't take your place." Lukas bumped shoulders with him.

"The team acquired you because you're versatile like me, which makes you more of an asset than Padraig." He tilted his head in Padraig's direction. "Being able to play different positions gives you a chance to be a great player."

He wasn't sure what Lukas was thinking while he studied him, but Ewansiha knew it didn't matter. He wouldn't be doing his team any good if he wasn't playing at a hundred per cent.

"I'll tell Coach," Sergio informed him, then patted him on the knee before he stood. "You need to stay off that knee for the rest of the match. We'll ice it tonight and put heat on it later."

Nodding, Ewansiha inhaled sharply. He'd known he wasn't going to play the entire match anyway, but he was disappointed that he couldn't have held out longer. After coming over, the coach frowned at him, then glanced over at Lukas.

"I guess you're taking Kroenig's place at the beginning of the next half, Schultz."

"Yes, sir."

So it starts.

No man could play football forever, and Ewansiha knew his time was running short in the game that he loved, but he hadn't thought it would happen quite this soon. Yet he couldn't think of another player he'd prefer to take his place on the team.

Oh, he wasn't going to give it up without a fight, but it might be something to think about as the season progressed. He'd have to keep an eye out on his knee to see how it held up to a full season of matches.

"I'm sorry," Lukas whispered as the coach walked away.

Ewansiha shook his head. "I just need a little more time to heal, I guess, and trust me, this isn't a permanent replacement."

Lukas' eyebrows shot up, and Ewansiha chuckled. *It's not going to be that easy, honey. I'm not going to roll over and let you take my spot just yet.*

"I got it." Lukas smiled.

"All right, gentlemen. Let's get our asses out there and win this match!" the coach yelled at them.

Ewansiha covered Lukas' hand, then squeezed quickly before anyone could notice. "You'll do great, and I'll be out to watch in a few."

Lukas nodded, then ran out with the rest of the team. Ewansiha rested his head back on the locker, tired and aching. He was more than ready to go soak his leg in some ice to dull the pain.

"How are things going between you?"

He peered at Sergio who walked over to him. Ewansiha held out his hand, and Sergio took it. Together, they got Ewansiha on his feet.

"It's going great." He glanced around, and saw that they were alone. After leaning down, he brushed his lips over Sergio's cheek in thanks. "I appreciate what you did to get us to stop being idiots."

"Darling, it wasn't a hardship for me to be the filling in a Lukas and King sandwich." Sergio winked. "Let's get you out to the bench. Oh, and here's some pain meds."

He dry-swallowed them, hoping they kicked in fast. "Sergio, I'm not sure if I'm going to make it through this season. I wasn't expecting it to be this bad still.

Maybe it's just time to start thinking about what's beyond football."

Sergio shook his head. "It's only the first match, honey. I'm positive that by the middle of the season, you'll be back to normal."

Ewansiha wasn't sure he believed what Sergio thought, but he wasn't going to discuss it with him.

He rode the bench for the rest of the match, and cheered as Lukas played almost as well as Ewansiha did at full speed. The young man just needed a few more years to gain experience and he'd be one of the great ones. He cheered as Padraig scored the tying goal.

As time wound down, the fans on both sides grew louder, and the atmosphere in the stadium grew desperate as each team tried to score. The goalies were putting on a show of amazing stops while the forwards were crashing into each other to get the ball.

Ewansiha knew something was going to break. After having seen years of football matches, he'd learnt how to tell which ones would end in a tie, and which ones would have a clear winner. This match had the feel of a clear winner. He just wasn't sure which team would come out on top.

Padraig raced towards the goal and the fans screamed his name. Ewansiha studied all the defenders, wishing he was out there so he could yell at Padraig to shoot the ball over to the left forward who had a clear path to the goalie. It was almost like Padraig heard what Ewansiha had been thinking.

Whirling around, Padraig drove the ball towards the other forward, who caught it in stride, then shot it at the goal. The other team's goalie reacted a second too late, and the ball hit the net with a thud.

Everyone went crazy because it was right then that the referee blew the whistle to stop the match. They had played an extra three minutes for stoppages and luck was on their side. Ewansiha wished he could join his teammates in their celebration, but he couldn't stand without help since his knee had stiffened up.

Lukas rushing up to him made Ewansiha worry that the man would forget where he was and kiss him, but Lukas skidded to a stop right in front of him. They smiled at each other, knowing they would be having their own personal celebration back at Ewansiha's house.

"Congratulations, King. We won our first match." Lukas helped Ewansiha to his feet, letting him lean against him as they made their way to the locker room.

"We did at that. It's a good omen for the rest of the season."

The noise from the locker room hit them like a wall as they opened the door to go in. Sergio immediately grabbed Ewansiha to lead him away to the stadium's sports medicine room.

"Come by and get me when you're ready to go?" Ewansiha asked as Lukas started to disappear into the other room.

"I will. Don't worry. I'm not going to leave you behind." Lukas flashed him another smile, then walked away.

Ewansiha sighed, feeling left out for the first time in his entire career, even though it wasn't the first time he'd gone to get patched up while the rest of his team congratulated each other on the win.

"Don't worry. You're still the King. None of them are going to forget you for a long time." Sergio grinned at him. "And Lukas isn't ever going to forget or leave you behind. You're it for him, I think."

"Thanks for stroking my ego, Serge." He laughed.

"That's all I can stroke now. Lukas would take my hand or head if I touched you anywhere around your groin."

Ewansiha met Sergio's knowing gaze. "That's pretty much how I feel about the two of you now as well. We're both off the market, I guess."

Sergio helped him sit on the table, then it was his turn to sigh. Ewansiha knew what had caused his friend to make that sound. He reached out to catch Sergio's hand. He brought it up to his lips before placing a kiss to Sergio's knuckles.

"Don't fret, honey. There's someone out there for you, and I have a feeling you're going to find him soon."

"I hope so. I'm not getting any younger." A slamming door caused Ewansiha to drop Sergio's hand as he jumped. Sergio huffed in amusement. "Let's get you soaking. It'll be a while before Lukas comes in. The coach will want to discuss what they did right, and I'm sure there'll be a reporter or two who wants to talk to him."

Ewansiha allowed Sergio to take over, knowing that he needed to be able to move better later than he did at the moment. He had plans for Lukas when they got back home.

Chapter Fourteen

A couple of matches later, the team entered the locker room in silence, displeasure at their loss evident in the tension filling the air. Ewansiha went to his locker then dropped onto the bench in front of it. His knee ached, and he knew the kick he'd received from his counterpart on the other team had bruised it. He just hoped it wasn't so bad that he couldn't play in the next match.

Padraig continued to rant about the opposing team's goalie as they undressed. "That fucking cocksucker cheated. I told the referees, but the fags didn't listen to me." His voice grew louder and louder until he filled the room with his anger.

Ewansiha tensed, having heard too many of Padraig's tantrums. He knew what was coming and he didn't know if he could take more of it, especially now that Lukas and he were seeing each other.

"I told the fag that if I saw him do that again, I'd tear his fucking bloody arm off and beat him about his cocksucking head with it." Padraig slammed his hand into the side panel of his locker. "I can't believe they let fags like him play. I mean really? He's got no talent. Must have blown someone to get on the team."

Ewansiha saw Lukas glance at him, and he could tell that his lover was worried about what he was going to do. Padraig uttered one more fag comment, which caused Ewansiha to throw his boot as hard as he could into his own locker. Everyone looked at him. Padraig stopped talking when Ewansiha stood then stalked over to him.

He poked Padraig in the chest. "I'm sick and tired of listening to your homophobic bullshit. Shut your bloody mouth until you've learnt how to respect others."

"What the hell?" Padraig shoved him away. "Don't touch me, and I can say whatever the hell I want."

"No, you can't. Not anymore. I'm telling you that, from now on, you will show respect for everyone in this locker room." Ewansiha wasn't about to out anyone, but he was fed up with Padraig being an asshole.

Shrugging, Padraig glanced around the room. "None of the boys care what I say. They feel the same way."

"They might, but I don't. You're a disrespectful wanker, Padraig, and I'm done listening to you going on about gays and calling people fags like being gay makes them less than human, or less of a footballer. I'm tired of hearing you go on about a man's sexuality, or his ethnicity, or who his mother might have been." He could see the confusion in Padraig's gaze and he realised he was starting to lose the man. Padraig was known more for reacting than thinking.

"Just stop using gay and racial slurs, and I'll leave you alone." Ewansiha turned to walk back to his locker.

"Why? Are you a fag, King?"

Sudden tension permeated the room, and he could almost sense the fear rolling off Lukas. While Ewansiha knew he only had three or four good years left in the league, Lukas had his entire career ahead of him. Being known as a gay footballer was becoming less and less of an issue every year—at least in the locker room—but fans and reporters weren't nearly as open-minded yet. They could be vicious and dangerous towards people they viewed as different.

Ewansiha would do everything in his power to keep Lukas safe, though he wasn't quite ready to lie entirely to do it. Lukas was a big boy. He could fight his own battles, but he probably would like to pick them himself.

Facing Padraig again, Ewansiha crossed his arms over his chest and stared at him. "Whether I am or not isn't the point. Whether anyone on this team is or not isn't the point. What the point is, is that we shouldn't be forced to endure uneducated rants from bigoted mouth-breathers like you. If we are to keep building a feeling of mutual respect and teamwork, then we shouldn't have to hear such negative things being said around us."

He wasn't expecting anyone to stand beside him in the argument. Most of the guys didn't want to deal with Padraig's obnoxious behaviour, so he was shocked when Paolo moved to his side.

"King's right, Paddy. You gotta watch what you say. Kids out there look up to you and when they hear you say shit like that, they think it's okay for them to say it." Paolo rested his hand on Padraig's shoulder. "Then those kids treat other kids like that. It's a vicious cycle, man, and we have to figure out how to break it."

Blinking, Ewansiha wondered where this Paolo had come from and who had switched them. Whatever Paolo's opinions had been before this, the man had never expressed them, and he was Padraig's best friend, so he should've been the one to say something earlier.

"But why would they think that?" Padraig looked puzzled. "And anyway, why shouldn't I speak up when I think something's wrong?"

"Because the way you do it encourages anger and hatred against people who aren't any different from you." Paolo took a deep breath then said, "If I told you I was gay, would it change how I play football? Would it change how you think of me, and what you thought you knew about me?"

Shocked silence reigned while Padraig's eyes widened. Ewansiha saw him pale.

"Are you?" Padraig whispered, and only Paolo and Ewansiha heard his question.

Paolo licked his lips, then shot Ewansiha a quick glance before he smiled slightly. "Nah, but see? My question got you thinking, didn't it, Paddy? That's all I'm asking at the moment. Just think before you speak."

Ewansiha wanted more than that. He wanted Padraig to stop saying the hateful words, but maybe Paolo was right. Maybe getting Paddy to think before he said something was a good start at getting him to change his ways.

Ewansiha went to his locker and grabbed his towel and kit before heading to the showers. He'd had his say—if Padraig wanted to continue the conversation, he could follow him into the showers. Something told him that Padraig wouldn't try to match wits with him.

What was that look Paolo gave me? Does he know about Lukas and me? At one point, before he'd started his relationship with Lukas, any of his teammates knowing he was into guys would've have scared him shitless. Now he was realising it didn't matter. He would deal with it if it ever came to light.

No one tried to strike up a conversation with him, and Lukas avoided him until they were ready to go. Ewansiha noticed Paolo kept close to Padraig, talking to him in quiet words. Who knew Paolo could be a steadying influence on Padraig?

He approached Lukas, then waited while his lover finished an interview with a local news reporter.

"Are you ready to head out?" Ewansiha asked while giving the reporter a brief nod.

"Yeah. Thanks for giving me a ride. I still need to get my car fixed." Lukas grabbed his backpack, then slung it over his shoulder.

Lukas' car being fixed had been their cover story for arriving at the stadium together for games and practices for the last week or so. Everyone knew they lived near each other, so it made sense for Ewansiha to give Lukas a lift.

It wasn't until they were in the car and on their way back to Ewansiha's that Lukas looked at him and said, "Are you out of your ever-loving mind?"

Ewansiha raised one shoulder, but didn't take his gaze from the road. "I couldn't take it anymore. I've been listening to Padraig rant and rave, calling the opposing team's players every racial slur he could think of, or calling them fags and poofs. I got tired of it, Lukas. How is the attitude and atmosphere in the sport ever going to change, if we don't take a stand and force the issue?"

"I appreciate you doing that, but you know what can happen to anyone who comes out. I don't need to be convinced any more that you're not ashamed of our relationship." Lukas reached out to rest his hand on Ewansiha's thigh. "It's not my fellow teammates I'm worried about. I'm worried about the assholes in the stands who call you nigger and monkey to your face. Those men are the kind who would hunt us down if they thought we were gay. They would try to kill us because we dare to be different."

"I didn't say we had to come out. All I'm saying is that we need to have a little respect in the locker room. It doesn't matter what he calls them, I don't want him to do it." He shook his head. "The sad thing is Padraig doesn't get it. He doesn't see anything wrong with calling people names or putting them down. Yet, I bet if I were to call him a poofter or a fag, he'd get in my face and try to kick my ass."

"Try being the operative word here. You'd crush him like the little bug he is." Lukas grinned at him, and Ewansiha realised he was trying to change the subject.

After taking a deep breath to bring his anger under control, he chuckled. "Padraig likes to talk a big game, but he knows I outweigh him and am taller than him. He might think he's a scrapper, but he hasn't been in the kind of fights I've been in."

Lukas leaned his head against the seat to study Ewansiha. "What was life like for you before you came to Germany? I know you lived in Nigeria with your mom until you were sixteen."

"My parents divorced when I was young, and Mom took me and my brothers back home to Nigeria with her. I was the youngest, but I was a hellion. Got in trouble every chance I got. Football was the only thing

I loved and wanted to do, but I couldn't do it twenty-four seven there." His mom had been a saint for all the stuff he'd put her through. "She finally had enough of me when I was sixteen. Sent me here to live with my dad and his new wife. She'd told him about how much I loved football, so he got me a try-out for one of the junior teams."

"And the rest, as they say, is history," Lukas murmured.

Oh, his career hadn't been a fairy tale. There had been injuries that had almost ended it before it'd even started, but he'd managed to bounce back to play at the high level needed in this league. Well, he had until this last injury, yet he understood it—he was getting older and it took longer for his body to heal.

"Right." He pulled into his driveway, then into the garage.

As they walked inside, Ewansiha gritted his teeth against the ache in his knee. He tried not to limp, but Lukas must have been paying closer attention than he'd thought.

"Why don't you go soak in the hot tub for a little bit? I'll make us something light for dinner. I have to check on Xav anyway." Lukas caressed his shoulder as he walked past him.

"Why don't you just go and get him? He can spend the night here if he wants."

Lukas froze where he stood in front of the refrigerator. "Are you sure? I didn't think you wanted anyone to know about us."

Ewansiha braced his body against the counter nearest him. The pain was getting worse, so he knew he was going to need some meds that night. "I don't care if he knows. He'll keep his mouth shut, right? Unless you don't care if he outs you to anyone."

"You're right, but he knows I'm gay. He doesn't know about you."

He rolled his eyes at that statement. "The kid isn't stupid, Lukas. He has to know something's going on between us. You've been staying over here a lot."

The dawning realisation of that fact on Lukas' face brought a smile to Ewansiha's face.

"Shit!" Lukas slammed the fridge door. "I've got to talk to him."

"Go get him and come back here. I don't care who knows among our friends, Lukas. I told you that before." He shuffled over to press a kiss to Lukas' cheek. "Take my car. I'll be soaking when you get back."

* * * *

All the way home, Lukas thought about what Ewansiha had said. He couldn't believe that after keeping his sexuality under wraps his whole career, he was willing to make exceptions to the 'don't tell' rule he'd lived by. Especially now that he had the perfect cover in the form of Silvia having his baby. You couldn't get more straight-seeming than knocking up your ex-girlfriend and claiming the child as your own.

Maybe when he'd said it was okay for their friends to know, he'd just meant Silvia and Xav and Sergio. Which would basically be the same people who'd known thus far, plus Xav. When it came right down to it, would Ewansiha want to go that extra step and own up to their relationship publicly? Even during the scene in the locker room, Ewansiha had stopped short of using his own sexuality to further his point to Padraig. Not that Lukas had expected him to, but didn't Ewansiha see that if they opened the door a crack, there was no telling who would end up finding out? And if he didn't care anymore, did that mean he thought his career was nearing its end?

Or that…his relationship with Lukas made it worth doing now?

Stop it. God, you're barely even dating. He's not going to make a life-altering decision because of you. Get over yourself.

Even if Ewansiha's career was almost done, he had his retirement to think about. Whether he had endorsements, or offers to coach, broadcast, give clinics or motivational speeches, it all depended on his having a good public image. And, sadly, some homophobic people had the power to affect the course of those things. They could easily view their relationship as deviant and Ewansiha unworthy of their consideration. Which was just a shame, since Ewansiha was one of the best people he'd ever known.

Lost in thought, he pulled Ewansiha's car into his driveway then stared in horror at the sight of Padraig and Paolo climbing out of Padraig's car. Paolo turned to him and made an uncertain gesture, looking uncharacteristically worried, then turned back to Padraig, who was still obviously upset from the game or the scene with King in the locker room, or both.

Lukas slammed the car into park, turned it off then jumped out. He hurried to try to intercept Padraig before he got to the door, but Paolo caught his arm.

"Sorry, man. I couldn't talk him out of coming here. What I said in the locker room about being a role model for kids got him all riled up and now he wants to spend time with Xav to convince me—and probably himself—that kids do like him and still look up to him."

"I do *not* want him around Xav when he's like this."
Lukas tore himself away from Paolo but it was too
late. Xav was already letting Padraig into the house
with a huge smile on his face. Padraig was grinning
back, though it looked less than genuine. Lukas
slowed his mad dash, hoping against hope that having
his ego stroked by Xav's hero worship would be
enough to talk Padraig off the ledge.

He crossed his fingers that the volatile forward
would have the social skills to keep his homophobic
mouth shut about those views around Xav.

Lukas walked straight to Xav and gave him a
backslapping hug. "Hey, Xav. Can I talk to you for a
sec?" He tried to steer Xav away, but he dug his heels
in.

"Oh, but these guys just got here..."

"What's the matter, Lukas? You think I'm an evil
influence on all future generations too?" Padraig's
grin had morphed into something more like a
grimace.

Xav frowned. "What? Evil influence?"

Fuck. Lukas tugged on his arm, but Xav refused to
move, his focus on Padraig.

"Oh yeah, apparently I'm not fit to be around kids
according to King and Paolo, and probably Lukas
too." Padraig glared at Lukas and Paolo, his face
growing red and a vein throbbing in his temple. He
glanced at Xav and visibly tried to get himself under
control. Lukas was glad to see that he was at least
making an effort.

Paolo was whispering urgently into his phone while
Padraig walked into the garage.

"What is going on?" Confusion clouded Xav's eyes.

"Sergio is almost here," Paolo interjected in a low
tone to Lukas.

"Why Serge?" Lukas didn't exactly want him subjected to Padraig's mood either.

"Haven't you noticed he's about the only one Padraig hears? Especially when he's all worked up."

"Besides you," Lukas reminded him. "You guys are best friends."

"Yeah, well, he's not listening to me today, obviously," Paolo pointed out and ran his hand through his hair.

"Will somebody tell me what's happening?" Xav's voice was getting louder and Lukas and Paolo both shushed him.

Padraig chose that moment to reappear with a football in his hands. "Think fast." He lobbed it at Paolo's head, and the goalie used his amazing reflexes to snatch it out of the air in spite of the phone he still held.

As Paolo tried to juggle the two without dropping either one, Padraig snagged the cell phone out of his hands. "Who the hell you talking to?" He glanced at the screen. "Sergi—o...?" He became deathly still, his eyes riveted to the screen. "What the fuck is that?" he muttered hoarsely.

"Oh shit." Paolo dropped the ball and practically tackled Padraig to fight for his phone.

"What?" Lukas didn't like the look on Padraig's face as he stayed eerily silent and worked to wrestle the phone back away from Paolo, who was uttering a steady stream of "Fuck, fuck, fuck, fuck..." as he made every effort to retrieve it.

Xav was pressed back against the counter watching the men.

Padraig won the fight for the phone with one last shove and pinned Paolo with a cold stare. "Just... Stop." He tapped and swiped his fingers across the touchscreen a few times, his expression growing grimmer and grimmer.

Lukas heard the front door and footsteps hurrying towards the doorway from the dining room. Unfortunately, Padraig was the closest to that part of the kitchen, so no one could intercept Sergio before he rounded the corner and came to an abrupt halt.

Padraig whipped his head around and stared at Sergio like he'd never seen him before. Lukas didn't know whether to wish Ewansiha was there—since he was the only one bigger than Padraig—or be glad that he didn't have to go through whatever was about to go down.

I don't know what the hell is going on, but shit, this could get ugly.

Chapter Fifteen

They all stood in a frozen tableau. Lukas had no idea what the hell was on Paolo's phone, but by the looks of it, it couldn't be good. Padraig was in another dimension with his rage. Paolo had his head clasped in his hands and Xav was watching them all with huge eyes from the corner of the counter.

Sergio looked at the phone outstretched towards him in Padraig's hand and pressed his lips together, shooting an irritated glance at Paolo, who mouthed, *"I'm sorry."* Lukas started to get a bad feeling about what sort of photo Paolo had on his phone.

"Sergio?" Padraig finally spoke, sounding weirdly calm. "Who is that?"

Sergio shook his head, not looking away from Padraig.

Padraig turned to Paolo. "Is it you?"

"Does it matter?" Paolo finally answered, sounding defeated.

"Fuck yes, it matters. It's bad enough that our trainer is a cocksucking fag"—Lukas heard Xav gasp and moved quickly to his side—"but I'm not fucking playing with one, being best mates with one, having one on the team…" His voice rose as he continued, "I want to know right now! Is it you?"

"It's not him," Sergio answered for a silent Paolo.

Padraig focused on Sergio and took a step forward. "Who is it?"

Sergio lifted his chin a touch. "None of your business."

Lukas' eyes widened at Sergio's bravado. A sudden movement caught his attention and he looked down at Xav in time to see him dash angrily at a tear trickling down his cheek. Betrayal and disillusionment already shone in his eyes, and Lukas knew he had to get him out of there before he saw more, or got involved in any way.

He muscled a resistant Xav towards the living room door, which soon drew everyone's attention. Sergio moved in their direction immediately, obviously understanding what Lukas was trying to do and why.

Paolo spoke up, sounding disgusted, "This goes along with what I meant earlier, Paddy. You think this kid is ever going to look at you with stars in his eyes again? You fucking ruined that for yourself and for him. He didn't need to hear that kind of shit from you."

"*You* shut up. We're not done talking about this, and *you*" —Padraig stepped up to block Sergio's path, chest bumping him—"you're a fucking perversion and you stay away from him. He's a good kid—"

"Leave him alone!" Xav screamed, tearing himself away from Lukas and running over to push Padraig away from Sergio. He fought the adults trying to pull him away and stood his ground between Padraig and Sergio. "You still gonna think I'm a good kid if I tell you I'm a fag too? Huh?"

Tears streamed heedless down his face as everyone in the room practically stopped breathing as they waited for Padraig's reaction. Lukas' heart was in his throat.

"Oh, I know guys like you," Xav whispered, his gaze locked on Padraig. "You hate yourself...so you pretend you hate us. Well fuck you. God, I looked up to you. What a crock of shit. Fuck you. Just... Fuck. You." Xav's strength finally seemed to run out. He slumped and allowed Lukas to pull him away from the confrontation, into the living room and into his arms.

Sergio and Paolo managed between them to herd a stunned Padraig out of the kitchen the other way, towards the front door. Lukas held a shaking Xav against his chest while Sergio and Paolo had a whispered conversation in the foyer.

Padraig stood like a statue, his stare bouncing between all of them in turn, probably not even aware that he was shaking his head slightly in disbelief.

Lukas knew what he had to do. He ushered Xav to the couch. "Stay here." Then he stalked over to the front door.

"Padraig." It appeared that all of the fight had gone out of the team captain as he met his gaze in response. *Good.* "Just so you know without a shadow of a doubt, *I* am gay... And you are never welcome in this house again. And if you try anything with either me or Sergio, or anyone else for that matter, I will do everything I can to make your life a living hell, after I have you prosecuted for a hate crime. Now, get out." Lukas opened the front door and stared Padraig down, pointedly waiting for him to move.

Padraig still looked shell-shocked, as though he'd woken up from a nightmare. He moved his gaze from Lukas to Paolo, who shook his head.

"Paolo?"

"No, Paddy. Just go."

Lukas watched as Padraig's disbelief grew at the defection of his best friend and he gathered the remnants of his self-righteousness around him like a cloak. His defensiveness manifested itself as anger and a sneer.

"Fine. Fuck you. If you want to stay here with these..." He trailed off as he glanced in Xav's direction. Then he shook his head sharply and stormed through the front door. He slammed it after him and a few moments later they heard him peel out of the driveway then gun his car up the street.

"God, I hope he doesn't kill anyone..." Sergio was pale as a ghost in the wake of the conflict. "Or himself," he added in a whisper.

"This was all my fault."

They all looked at Paolo. "What?" Lukas asked incredulously. "How can you say any of this was your fault?"

"Paolo..." Sergio started to soothe.

"I should've deleted that picture, not made it your contact photo. What the fuck was I thinking?" Paolo looked miserable.

Lukas warred for a moment in his head then, in spite of himself, came out with, "Okay, I hate to even ask, but... What the hell was in the picture?"

Paolo widened his eyes and jerked his head at Xav then shook it.

"Oh, come on. I'm sixteen, not six. You don't have to *show* it to me, but I want to know what made him freak out so bad." Xav turned around on the couch to kneel on the cushion and rest his arms on the back while his eyes pleaded with Paolo. Lukas marvelled at the resilience of the young man. "It'll cheer me up," he persisted.

Sergio laughed and the mood in the room lightened considerably. "Well, let's just say I had a close-up taken with a very nice dancer who was sporting our team colours on an interesting part of his body. And no, I wasn't doing anything but smiling for the camera. Well… *Something* was kind of touching my cheek, but it was hard to get it in the frame with my face otherwise. And maybe I had my tongue… Anyway, I sent it to Paolo that night. And he evidently *kept* it." This was said with a stern look at Paolo. "Did I or did I not tell you you'd better get that off your phone? With the amount of time you spend with Padraig—"

"Why didn't you send it to me?" Lukas blurted out without thinking, though he wondered what the hell it said about him that he felt left out for not getting the cock shot.

Sergio raised an eyebrow at him in amusement. "It was from before you joined the team, hon."

"I changed my mind, can I see it?" came from the couch.

"No," all three men said at once.

Xav huffed with a disgruntled look on his face, then spun around, landing on his butt. They all laughed. Lukas spotted the discarded football and rolled it up his leg to get it off the floor. He kicked it up in the air a couple of times before passing it to Paolo, who caught with his chest then grabbed it in his hands.

"By the way, Lukas—you do realise you just came out to the team…or at least the team captain?

Congratulations." Sergio winked at Lukas, who absorbed that fact with a jolt.

"Well... So did you," he countered.

"True. I feel so liberated." He smiled. "C'mon, Paolo, I'll give you a ride home." Sergio bumped his shoulder.

Paolo paled. "Maybe I should've taken my chances with Paddy. Or... Say, I could drive your car."

"Oh, whatever. I'm not *that* bad of a driver," Sergio protested on their way out of the door. Paolo turned at the last second and pitched the ball to Lukas then winked as he shut the door behind them.

Lukas turned to Xav. "So, I was wondering if, instead of staying here while I'm gone tonight, you wanted to come with me."

"To King's house?"

"Yeah."

"You guys are together, huh?"

Smart kid. "Yeah."

Xav appeared to think about that for a moment then shrugged his thin shoulders. "That's okay with him if I come over?"

"He's the one who suggested it." Lukas thought for a moment. "He has a hot tub. And an amazing game station set-up."

"In that case, I'll pack. Let's just move in," Xav joked as he stood. His smile faded a bit. "Thanks for sticking up for me...again."

Lukas' chest tightened as he wondered at how quickly Xav had come to mean so much to him. "Always. Now let's go."

* * * *

Ewansiha finally got too hot to stay in the hot tub any longer. How long should it have taken for Lukas to get to his place, talk to Xav, grab a few things and come back? He had no clock handy and he'd sort of dozed off, so he wasn't sure exactly how long Lukas had been gone, but it seemed like it had been a while.

He stepped out and dried off then wrapped a towel around his waist. Maybe it was a good thing they hadn't come back yet, actually. He wasn't in the habit of wearing anything in the hot tub—living alone and having a private yard meant he didn't have to worry about it—so he'd have to change his habits if Xav was going to be a frequent visitor…

Or more.

He knew it was a bit early to be thinking about living together with Lukas, but by the same token, they'd known each other for years already—knew each other's good qualities and quirks. They'd just added a new and amazing dimension to a well-established friendship.

Ewansiha half expected to hear Lukas pulling into his garage when he walked in the house, but nothing. Starting to worry, he checked the time and realised that over an hour had gone by. Unease pricked at his chest. No messages either. Something must have gone wrong. Maybe Xav had taken the news badly and Lukas had changed his mind? Or could he have got in an accident?

He debated for a moment then dialled Lukas' home number first. No answer. Rather than leave a message he hung up and was about to dial his cell when he heard the very welcome sound of his garage door going up. Letting out a gusty sigh of relief, he crossed the kitchen to the garage door and opened it.

Lukas gave him a finger wave from atop the steering wheel as he finished pulling in and parking. Once the engine noise was gone, Ewansiha called out, "I'll be right back down. Just going to get dressed."

"Okay," Lukas replied as he got out of the car. He looked tired, and so did Xav, who was looking around the garage instead of at him.

Ewansiha mouthed, *"Everything okay?"* to Lukas, who silently replied, *"Later."*

Damn. The talk with Xav must not have been fun.

Ewansiha hurried upstairs to change, relieved that his knee seemed to have benefited from the extended period of time in the hot tub. He took a quick shower and, after a mental debate, hastily dressed in his usual comfortable around-the-house clothes instead of dressing in nicer, have-company clothes.

By the time he got downstairs, Xav and Lukas were side by side in his kitchen, cooking something. "That smells delicious, whatever it is," he said by way of greeting. Xav glanced over his shoulder with a shy smile then returned to pushing some colourful vegetables around in a sauté pan. Lukas placed the cutting board and a knife in the sink, washed his hands then turned to smile at him.

"You okay to finish up while I have a quick chat with Ewansiha?" he asked Xav. "Just cook them until they're forkable then toss in the chopped tomatoes. And the pasta's easy, just make sure to set the timer."

"Yeah, I got this. Go fill him in on the big scene he missed. I don't mind missing the instant replay of that." As Ewansiha walked towards the living room, he heard Xav mumble, "Wish I could've missed it the first time around."

Lukas hesitated when they got to the living room and Ewansiha took him by the hand, sat on the couch and tugged him down next to him.

"What's this all about? What big scene?" Rather than let go, he twined their fingers together, not missing the squeeze Lukas gave his hand in return.

Lukas gave a short laugh. "It was... I don't know where to start. Maybe I'll get into all the details another time, but I'm with Xav—I just don't even want to go there right now."

Ewansiha was about to burst with frustration at not knowing, then Lukas continued, "But basically... Padraig and Paolo were there when I got home and Xav invited Padraig in. He was still really wound up from the scene with you earlier, but even so, at first it seemed like things would be okay."

"All right," Ewansiha encouraged, knowing that that was probably the best of what was to come.

"Paolo had called Sergio to have him come help out with getting Padraig calmed down, and, well..." Lukas inexplicably smiled.

"What?"

Lukas started shaking and at first Ewansiha was worried, then he figured out it was with repressed laughter. "Paolo had a picture of Sergio with a cock practically in his face as his contact photo... I don't know why I'm laughing." He took a deep breath. "Padraig saw it and went ballistic. He flipped out just as Serge got there."

Oh no. "Oh God. Why didn't you call me?" And here he'd been lounging in the hot tub.

Lukas shook his head and continued, "After that, Padraig predictably started with his 'fag' bullshit. Sergio stood up to Padraig and basically outed himself, then Xav got involved—"

"Wait... He was right there?"

"Oh yes." Lukas smiled but it was sad. "He shoved Padraig away from Serge and told him he was a 'fag' too. He was so brave." His eyes glinted for a moment and he blinked. "Anyway, I kicked Padraig out... Told him I'm gay and he's never welcome – Ouch."

Ewansiha realised he was squeezing the hell out of Lukas' hand and let go. "Sorry." He cradled Lukas' head between his hands and met his gaze. "You outed yourself to Padraig?" On the one hand, he was so proud of his lover for defending Xav and Sergio by revealing his own orientation. On the other, he was terrified for Lukas' safety and his career.

Lukas nodded. "I...just had to right then. You know?" Emotional reaction swelled in his eyes and Ewansiha pulled him into his embrace. "I didn't say anything about you or us, and it's none of his business anyway." He swallowed against Ewansiha's neck. "Maybe it's naive but I don't think Padraig is going to say or do anything. He'll hate us, but... I don't know. Maybe I'm wrong." He pulled back. "I guess what I'm saying is, no more grand gestures in front of the team by either of us. We'll just live our lives and if things blow up later on, we'll handle what comes." He shrugged and looked down at his hands. "Is that a cop-out? I just don't want another scene and I don't want to fuck up the rest of your career and retirement."

There was so much to think about that Ewansiha just spoke from his heart. "We'll take each day as it comes. And that's not a cop-out. That's just us living our lives. We'll take care of each other, our friends and Xav, and the rest will take care of itself."

It had seemed like the right thing to say and Lukas visibly relaxed.

"Let's go see how dinner's coming."

* * * *

That night, with Xav happily camped out downstairs playing a video game and a promise that he wouldn't stay up *too* late, Ewansiha and Lukas closed the door to his bedroom suite.

"Alone at last."

Lukas burst out laughing at the cheesy line, just as Ewansiha had intended. They'd had a nice evening together with Xav, but Ewansiha could occasionally see Lukas churning over the events of the day in his mind.

Now, he just wanted to make Lukas forget all his worries for the rest of the night.

They were still wet and warm from the hot tub and Ewansiha reached out to grab Lukas' towel while sending his own cascading to the floor. It wasn't quite the dramatic reveal it might have been, since they'd worn shorts in deference to Xav's presence, but Ewansiha still appreciatively eyed Lukas and the way the nylon shorts clung to his form.

He worked his way out of his own shorts and picked up the towels, then held out a hand. "Don't be shy," he teased.

Lukas grinned and turned around before wiggling out of the clinging garment. *Oh God, that ass.* Pale and muscular, concave at the sides, it tempted him whether clothed or unclothed.

Rather than face Ewansiha, Lukas tossed the wet item in a surprise move over his shoulder, forcing Ewansiha to grab to catch it. Then he sauntered across the room to Ewansiha's bed, making sure to put his backfield in motion, as the song went.

"Tease." Ewansiha smiled as he walked to the bathroom to hang the stuff in the shower.

"I'm only a tease if I don't follow through," Lukas called, now on his bed.

"And do you?" Ewansiha's cock was hardening the closer he got to Lukas.

"Do I what?"

"Plan to follow through?" Ewansiha crawled onto the mattress and lowered himself over Lukas.

"Oh, yesss..." Lukas inhaled sharply as their erections brushed. He wrapped his arms around Ewansiha and adjusted his legs to cradle him.

Ewansiha wasted no time in claiming a kiss as Lukas set up a rocking motion beneath him. He stroked his tongue into Lukas' yielding mouth and tried to keep up.

"Shh, there's no rush," he soothed when Lukas became nearly frantic beneath him.

"Speak for yourself," Lukas panted. He gave Ewansiha a gentle shove and once he was out of the way, got the lube from the drawer.

When it became clear that Lukas was going to prep himself with or without his involvement, he took over and made short work of opening up his impatient lover.

"Come on, big guy. Fuck me."

Ewansiha sucked in a breath at the graphic invitation. He grabbed a condom and eventually got it rolled on with his shaking hands, having evidently caught the same fever that was gripping Lukas.

Much as he loved looking at that ass, this time he wanted to watch Lukas' face. He grasped his hips to pull Lukas towards him and braced his thigh up on his to lift his ass slightly. After one last application of lube to his condom-covered erection and to Lukas' hole, he nudged into his entrance.

His eyes drifted closed at the perfect, tight feel of Lukas around him and he rocked forward a bit. Ewansiha forced his eyes open to meet Lukas' intent gaze. His mouth was parted and his lips swollen from their frantic kissing. He was pulling on his own cock. Ewansiha ran his hand along Lukas' smooth chest as he slowly worked his way into Lukas. When he tweaked his nipple, there was a corresponding contraction around his cock. He grinned and did it again.

"Fuck." Lukas arched his neck back, pressing his chest farther towards Ewansiha's hand.

"Yeah," Ewansiha encouraged then replaced Lukas' hand with his own and massaged his erection in time with his movements.

Lukas changed the angle slightly and braced his feet on the mattress, using his powerful body to more than meet every one of Ewansiha's thrusts.

His cock hardened impossibly in Ewansiha's hand. He spat to add slickness to the pre-cum and stroked him hard, tightening his hand around Lukas until he cried out. He spurted ropes of creamy white cum across his abdomen and Ewansiha's hand. As he did so, his passage clenched and Ewansiha was coming. He released Lukas' cock, grabbed his thighs and pounded into Lukas a few more times as he rode out his own climax.

Ewansiha lowered himself carefully onto Lukas' body and slowly rocked against him as his aftershocks waned. This time their kiss was tender and clinging. Ewansiha hated to have to move away to clean up. After he withdrew and stood to take care of the condom, he held a hand down to Lukas.

"Shower together? Then we can go to sleep."

A smile spread across Lukas' lips. "That sounds perfect."

Chapter Sixteen

The next morning, Lukas was in the kitchen making breakfast for him and King. Xav had left not long ago to go clothes shopping with Sergio. The team had the day off since they were travelling tomorrow for a series of away games, so he and King were having a lazy day while Sergio spent it breaking Lukas' bank account outfitting the growing kid with more than just T-shirts and sweats.

He got into a rhythm chopping vegetables for the frittata. He'd found he loved cooking when it was more than just him eating the food. That was one of the nice things about having Xav stay with him—it gave him an excuse to try new recipes. He also loved how Xav was so interested in learning to cook. And adding Ewansiha to the mix expanded things considerably. He wasn't much of a cook and was so appreciative of everything they prepared, it made Lukas want to impress him with good, healthy dishes.

When he heard the front door open, he glanced in that direction, wondering who it might be. Maybe Sergio and Xav had forgotten something?

"Ewansiha, where are you?"

Lukas flinched at the sound of a female voice. *Thank God I dressed before I came downstairs. Be embarrassing to be caught naked in King's kitchen.* He was pretty sure it was Silvia. Aside from King's mom, who wasn't in the country at the moment, he couldn't think of any other female who would just walk into Ewansiha's house without knocking first.

He turned off the stove, then set the knife he held on the counter before wandering out to the foyer. Lukas wasn't exactly looking forward to seeing her face to face for the first time since he'd started to date King. It didn't matter what King had told him about Silvia and him just being friends. He knew that if they did end up having a child together, the bond between them would be much more special, and a part of him was still afraid that at some point he would lose King to her.

The shower turned off upstairs, and Lukas heard the bedroom door open a few seconds later.

"Ewansiha, you better get your big black ass down here!" Silvia shouted. "I've got news!"

Lukas couldn't believe such a loud sound could come out of such a slender body. He walked out to see Silvia standing at the bottom of the stairs, staring up to where Ewansiha would be appearing soon.

He cleared his throat, and she whirled to look at him. Her eyes widened, but before she could say anything, King came to stand at the top of the stairs.

"I'm pretty sure that was a racist thing to say, Sil." He tugged on the T-shirt he'd been carrying before continuing, "And my ass is not big."

Silvia grinned as she winked at Lukas. "It'd only be racist if I were white, and since I'm not, I can say what

I want to you. When did you turn into a girl and start worrying about the size of your ass?"

"Probably comes from hanging out with you and your model friends too much. All I hear about is how fat you all are. Makes me sick."

Lukas watched as King descended the stairs. He was moving stiffly, so Lukas assumed that he hadn't taken his pills yet. When King drew Silvia into a tight hug and kissed her, Lukas turned away, not wanting to see that.

"Do you want to eat with us?" Lukas' question came out a little more tersely than he'd wanted.

"I'll just have a cup of coffee. You wouldn't happen to have any decaf, would you, Ewansiha?"

Ewansiha chuckled. "I might have herbal tea. My stepmom likes to drink it, so I make sure to have some on hand for her."

Lukas went back to the kitchen, glad for a reason to escape and not expecting them to follow him. He thought they would go into the living room for privacy. Yet they came in and took seats at the table in the breakfast nook while he heated the water for the tea. As he finished the food, they chatted.

"What did you want to tell me that you had to invade my house at some ungodly hour of the morning?"

Silvia's unladylike snort brought a reluctant smile to Lukas' face. "Invade? It wasn't like the two of you were still rolling around in bed or anything, Ewansiha. I knew you'd be up by now, even if Lukas had stayed over."

For some reason, Silvia's matter-of-fact comments about them having sex caused Lukas to blush and his face felt like it was on fire. Christ! He hadn't blushed like that since his mother had found him kissing Hans Gottfried in their basement when they were fifteen.

"Sil, you're shameless. Try not to embarrass Lukas so much that he runs away. I really like this one, and I'm not going to let you scare him off."

Lukas jerked his head up to stare in surprise at King. He'd known he meant something to the man because Lukas had got the feeling that Ewansiha didn't do casual flings, but he didn't know he'd stick up for him with Silvia.

"Oh come on, Ewansiha. He's not a kid. He knows I don't mean anything by it." She flashed a bright smile of thanks in Lukas' direction when he set her tea in front of her.

Her expression was friendly, and the vibe he'd received from her since she'd first seen him was open and accepting. Maybe what King had told him about them being only friends was true.

"Are you going to answer my question? What did you need to tell me?" King nodded his thanks to Lukas when he placed his coffee in front of him. Before he could walk away, King grabbed his wrist. "Make yourself a plate, Lukas, and join us."

While he bristled a little bit at the command in King's voice, Lukas was glad that he wanted him to sit at the table with them. He hurried to fill a plate, then sat next to King. A small smile crossed Silvia's face when King leaned over to brush a kiss over his lips.

"Thanks for breakfast, babe."

Lukas blinked at the endearment, but just said, "You're welcome."

"All right, now you're just making me sick. Too much sugar, Ewansiha, and you know what sugar does to me." Silvia shook her head.

"Quit teasing us, Sil, and tell me why you're here at this God-awful hour?" King held up a fork to keep her from commenting. "And it *is* a God-awful hour for you unless you're at a shoot."

"I'm going to have to get used to being up at this hour and earlier." She practically bounced in her chair. "The doctor called me, Ewansiha. We're going to be parents."

Lukas felt like someone had punched him in the stomach. Of course. *God, she's really going to have his baby.*

"That's great news, Silvia. When do you find out what you're having?" King seemed excited, but not nearly as thrilled as Lukas had thought he'd be.

Well, he did tell you the baby wasn't for him. Silvia wants one, so he gave her some of his sperm to make one. Still, it would be his son or daughter…

Lukas cleared his throat, and both of them turned to look at him. "Congratulations?"

Silvia reached across the table to take his hand then she squeezed it. "Thank you. That means a lot to me since I know you don't really understand why I asked Ewansiha to do this for us."

"Us?" His stomach dropped. That was just what he'd feared. King might not be using 'we' and 'us', but Silvia was. He attempted to hide his worry behind naivety. "He just explained that you're his best friend, and having a baby means so much to you. I get that, and I can't be such a bastard that I resent that. I have to admit that I'm pretty impressed that you want to go this alone."

Silvia's eyes narrowed as she glared at King. "You didn't tell him the whole story, did you?"

King shrugged, not taking his eyes off his plate. "It's not my story to tell, Silvia. I'm not going to share your personal life with others."

"But I told you to tell him *everything*."

Lukas felt his mouth drop open when she let go of his hand to smack King upside the head.

"Stop being an idiot. If Lukas is going to be a major part of your life, then he's going to be a big part of mine, and he needs to know all of the story."

"All of the story?" Lukas twisted to stare at King. "What does she mean by that exactly?"

King sighed, obviously feeling very put upon by them ganging up on him, and rolled his eyes. "Silvia is in a committed relationship with someone else," King announced before stuffing a forkful of eggs in his mouth.

"You're impossible." Silvia smacked him again. She turned to look at Lukas. "I've been in a relationship with Wendy Sarinova for years."

Stunned, Lukas had no idea what to say. Silvia was with another woman? For years. He cleared his throat. "You're kidding me!" That had been an idiotic thing to say, but it was the best he could do.

The situation began to finally process in his head. King wasn't having a baby with his ex-girlfriend. He was fathering a child for his lesbian best friend and her partner. Now that all the cards were on the table, Lukas felt with certainty for the first time that King *was* able to fully pursue a relationship with him, hopefully long term.

He began to smile at the joy of it all.

Ewansiha couldn't believe Silvia was telling Lukas when she wouldn't tell anyone else. Well, that wasn't true. She had told her parents, but no one else in her family knew about her and Wendy. Yet she was willing to spill the entire story to Lukas, all because Ewansiha had mentioned how much he liked him.

The conversation they'd had at the doctor's the other day while waiting for her to get impregnated jumped into his head. She'd asked him about Lukas, and he'd hemmed and hawed, not wanting to admit how much he enjoyed being with Lukas.

Yet she had somehow figured it out, and, being a woman, she knew that Lukas needed to know about what was going on with her and him. The tabloids were going to have a field day with the news of her pregnancy, and they would probably name him as the father.

She'd given him permission to tell Lukas everything, but Ewansiha had decided to omit a few things—like her and Wendy being a couple. As he had said before, it wasn't his secret to tell.

"All right, since Ewansiha seems to be very reluctant about the whole thing, I'll tell you." Silvia took a sip of her tea. "I was the one who helped Ewansiha to admit that he was bi. I recognised it because I'm bi as well. After we stopped dating, I never really found anyone worth being exclusive with, and neither did Ewansiha. So when we needed a date, we always called each other."

Ewansiha jumped when Lukas rested his hand on his thigh. He looked up to meet Lukas' eyes, worried that his lover would be angry with him for not telling him everything. There was understanding in Lukas' gaze, and joy almost overwhelmed the first emotion.

"You're such a private person. You never really thought that I might like to know that Silvia is in a committed relationship, and that it wouldn't matter whether it was with a man or a woman."

Blinking, he realised that he had never even considered that Lukas might still have felt insecure about their relationship. He covered Lukas' hand where it lay on his thigh before leaning over to kiss him hard.

"I'm sorry. I seriously never thought it mattered. As long as Sil and I weren't *together* together, I didn't think you'd care about whether she was seeing anyone." He ducked his head for a second. "I can't help but be protective of those I love."

Lukas cleared his throat. "Those you love?"

"Oh!"

Ewansiha looked over to see Silvia sitting there with her hand over her mouth and tears in her eyes. Panic set in, and he started to push to his feet. "Are you okay? Do we need to take you to the doctor's?"

She shook her head then wiped her eyes. "No. I'm just so happy that you found someone to love. Our family is getting bigger, Ewansiha, and in nine months, there'll be another life added."

Relaxing back in his chair, he nodded. "Where are you and Wendy going to live once the baby comes? And are you going to work up until you're showing?"

"No. I'm finishing up my last contract within the month, then I won't work until after the baby's here. We really haven't decided where we want our home to be. Neither one of us has strong ties to our own families." She held out her hand to Ewansiha, who took it. He was surprised when she did the same to Lukas, and he smiled when his lover entwined his fingers with hers.

"You're my family, Ewansiha, and Wendy feels the same way. This baby is yours as much as it is ours, and we want you to be in its life as a father. I'd love to stay here, so we can all be close." She pursed her lips.

"I'll talk to Wendy. We could probably find a place close to you."

"Why don't you move in here?" Both Silvia and Lukas stared at him. "What? It makes sense. It keeps the reporters off all of us. They'll never think that Lukas and I are a couple or that you and Wendy are if our lives are all interwoven."

"You're that worried about someone finding out about us?" Lukas sounded hurt.

"Not because I don't want anyone to know. I don't want to ruin the long career you have in front of you. I especially don't want to risk something happening to either one of us because some crazed fan gets worked up against gays." He took a deep breath, trying to calm his racing heart at the thought of something happening to Lukas.

Lukas wrapped one of his arms around Ewansiha's shoulder, tugging him close. They kissed again, then Lukas pulled back enough to rest his forehead against Ewansiha's.

"Thank you for making me one of those people you love enough to worry about."

"Always," he whispered.

They broke apart when the front door opened, and they heard someone running towards the kitchen.

"Lukas, are you down here?" Xav skidded around the corner into the kitchen, where he stopped so suddenly he almost fell over. His wide-eyed gaze landed on Silvia. "Oh my God! It's you."

Silvia stood gracefully, then approached Xav. She hugged him, and Ewansiha thought the boy's mouth was going to hit the floor. "You must be Xavier. I've heard some wonderful things about you."

"She has?" Lukas whispered in Ewansiha's ear.

"Yeah, I told her a little bit about him while we were at the doctor's the other day," he admitted. "I figured if we were all going to be friends together, she'd probably meet him at some time."

"Silvia, you gorgeous woman. Come give me a hug." Sergio swept in behind Xav, arms open to accept Sil's warm embrace. "You positively glow. Do you have good news?"

"Yes, it's very good news, but I'll let Ewansiha tell you. I have to get back to the Islands to finish up my photo shoot. I'll call you when I land." She blew him a kiss, then showed herself out.

"Oh my God!"

"You already said that, Xav," Lukas teased. "If I didn't know better, I'd think you had a crush on her."

"A man can be gay and still appreciate a beautiful woman," Xav said, then stuck his tongue out at Lukas.

"You're going to have to get used to having her around. She's part of the family now." Ewansiha picked up his fork. He wanted to finish his breakfast before things got crazier around his house. Yet he wasn't complaining.

For too long it had just been him rummaging around the place, and he'd been so private about his personal life that at times he'd isolated himself from people who could have been friends. No more of that.

He was going to dive head first into the relationship with Lukas and not care where it might lead him. They would deal with everything one day at a time, and if Padraig caused any problems, Ewansiha would straighten him out.

"Are you going to show me what you and Sergio bought?" Lukas asked Xav.

And the kid was off and running, his mouth going a mile a minute as he told them about the shops they'd gone to, and how much fun he'd had. Sergio and Lukas teased the teenager, and they all laughed.

Ewansiha smiled, liking the sound of laughter filling his house. *This is what family sounds like.*

Chapter Seventeen

"Lukas!" Xav yelled from downstairs.

Lukas didn't have the breath to answer him at the moment. He gritted his teeth and strained to keep from losing it.

"I'm there!" Ewansiha called, to his relief.

Lukas was shoulder to shoulder with Sergio, trying to keep from dinging up the walls along the staircase, while not getting squashed like a bug by the incredibly heavy, carved maple desk they were moving upstairs. Ewansiha was finally on the landing, so they made one last burst of effort and were able to set down the offending piece of furniture.

"On second thought, maybe it would be better off downstairs in the den?"

All three sweaty men swivelled to look at Silvia in disbelief.

She smirked. "Gotcha." She ran a hand over her still-flat stomach in what was fast becoming a habit. "Thank you so much for doing this. It means so much to us." Tears filled her eyes and Lukas panicked at the thought of being on the receiving end of yet another roller coaster emotional outburst from the hormonal woman. Sweetness and happy tears sometimes morphed straight into upset, pissed off ones, so it was time for a strategic retreat. Ewansiha's eyes begged him not to go, but it was every man for himself.

"I have to go see what Xav needs. Be back." He was already halfway down the stairs with Sergio hot on his heels.

"What was your excuse?" he half-whispered to Serge.

"I'm just the hired help. I don't need an excuse," he retorted.

Xav was practically dancing in the foyer.

"What's up?" Lukas asked him.

"There's photographers outside. They're taking pictures and everything. They even took a picture of me."

Lukas had known it was just a matter of time before the paparazzi sniffed out the story about Silvia moving into King's house.

"About time they got here," Sergio grumbled.

Lukas raised an eyebrow at him.

"Seriously. I tipped them off this morning. You'd think I wasn't a reliable anonymous source or something." He sounded quite put out.

"Okay, well, they're here now," he soothed the irritated Spaniard, who was muttering under his breath. Lukas was glad Xav didn't understand Spanish.

"Yes, true. I'll go gather up the mama-to-be and have her carry something very light and baby-oriented inside so they can get their shots and buzz off."

"Grab Ewansiha too. They'll want some of them both together." He unapologetically threw his lover under the bus. Sergio and Xav both grinned at him and he reflected on how their unconventional family just kept getting closer and closer. And it would be growing even more soon. Wendy's things were also being moved in today, though she had work to keep her busy over the coming months, so it would be more of a place to visit than a home until closer to the due date. Then the baby would be here…

And Ewansiha wouldn't be. Satisfaction flooded through Lukas at how happy he'd been a couple of weeks ago when Ewansiha had 'moved in' with him to leave his house free for the pregnant couple.

Xav had been supportive of his and King's relationship, but Lukas had been able to tell that he was uncomfortable with the idea of moving into King's house along with the women. Lukas had been torn between King and Xav and had dreaded bringing Xav's reluctance up to Ewansiha, who had been excitedly talking about them living together. But when he'd finally broached the topic, Ewansiha had surprised him.

"I'll just move into your house then." He'd cupped Lukas' jaw. "It doesn't matter to me where we live as long as we're together."

"But your beautiful house…" Lukas had protested.

King had shaken his head. "It's just a house. Maybe, if you're not too attached to yours, we can sell that one and move to something a bit bigger, with room for Xav and the baby. And maybe a hot tub." They'd laughed together. "We have time to figure it out."

* * * *

Later that evening, the guys were out on the deck enjoying their beverage of choice while Silvia was upstairs lying down in what was now her master suite while on the phone with Wendy before hopefully drifting off and getting a well-deserved nap in.

"I think…" Ewansiha started to speak, then paused, his focus on Lukas. "I mean, this is maybe a conversation we should have privately, but Xav and Serge are close to us so…"

A bit concerned, though he wasn't reading any worry in Ewansiha's face, Lukas leant forward and took his hand. "I'm sure it's fine. What's up?"

Ewansiha gave him that smile he loved. "I've had a great career…"

Lukas felt his eyes widen as he anticipated where this was going. Both Sergio and Xav were barely breathing.

"But I'm getting tired of fighting my knee and the last thing I want to do is cripple myself. I had always thought I'd play until I couldn't anymore and they hauled me off the field one last time." He smiled and Lukas had to give a slight laugh. He knew that feeling well. "Now, though, I have more in my life than football. You and Xav, Sil and the baby. I'm not saying I'm going to retire now, or even after this season, but"—he took a deep breath—"it's probably going to happen within the next season or so."

Ewansiha looked around at the rapt group before returning his gaze to Lukas. Lukas admired his calm expression, though who knew how he felt deep down?

"Mostly, I want to choose when I go out, not have my body make the choice for me." *Is that okay?* Ewansiha's eyes seemed to ask Lukas.

He started nodding and Ewansiha's expression reflected his relief at Lukas' support.

"I completely understand," he managed to say through the lump in his throat.

"That makes you head and shoulders smarter than most of the guys I've seen over the years," Sergio added. Then he sighed deeply.

Ewansiha and Lukas exchanged a glance. "Serge?" Lukas prodded.

Sergio gave them a sad smile. "Just keep me in the loop, hon," he said to Ewansiha, "because I'm only staying around as long as you're here. After all, someone has to keep your knee from exploding."

"What do you mean?" Surprisingly, the question came from Xav, who had been silently following along to that point.

"I've wanted to move on for a while now. Maybe back closer to home—Spain, Portugal... France, even. But I didn't want to leave you in the lurch at the end of your career. And... Well, he—" He froze and abruptly cut himself off. Lukas had never seen Sergio look so uncomfortable.

"He?" This from Ewansiha. "Have you been seeing someone?"

Sergio shook his head. "No. You'd know if I had, right?" He looked around at each of them and reluctantly smiled. "The looks on your faces right now. Fine. There was someone I'd had hopes for, but it became very clear recently that it's unrequited. So besides you guys, I have nothing to keep me here any longer." With that, Sergio sat back in his chair, and it was evident from his expression that he was done spilling his secrets. Lukas wondered who had their normally unflappable Sergio so unsettled.

A pounding accompanied the ringing of the doorbell and Lukas jumped up along with everyone else. "Christ. They're gonna wake Silvia up." And none of them wanted that.

He didn't wait but jogged to the front door just as it rang again. "Coming!" he called irritably and threw the door open. "Someone's sleeping, you…" He trailed off at the sight of who was on their doorstep. Instinctively he moved to block the man from stepping into the house. "Can I help you?"

"I want to talk to Xavier. I know he's here." The man bristling in front of him was practically Xav's twin, though on a bigger scale. Lukas now knew what Xav would look like in a few years. Their colouring and faces were nearly identical, but whereas Xav was still growing, this guy was several inches taller and clearly older, though still younger than Lukas.

"How you got that idea I'd like to know," Lukas prevaricated, honestly curious about it anyway. He tried to send a telepathic vibe to Xav to stay in the kitchen.

"A friend of a friend saw him in front of this house on the Internet earlier today. Now, are you going to get him for me or do I have to come in and find him myself?"

"What would you want with him?" Lukas stalled, trying to think of a good way to figure out what this guy's intentions were without giving away that Xav was actually there.

"Yeah. What do you want with me, Nik? I figured you never wanted to see my face again."

Lukas glanced over his shoulder and saw Xav staring at his brother with his jaw clenched and hands in fists. He was flanked protectively by Sergio and Ewansiha. "Xav? Should I let him in or close the door? You don't have to talk to him."

"If you think you're —" Nik began to protest.

"He can come in," Xav interrupted. "I really don't give a fuck what he has to say, but if it gets this over with any sooner, fine."

Lukas stepped back to allow Nik across the threshold into the foyer then closed the door. Lukas made no move to go elsewhere in the house and neither did anyone else.

"Well? What's so important you had to come all the way across town?"

Lukas started at that. He'd never really delved into Xav's past, respecting his wish not to talk about it, but he'd had no idea that his family was right here in this city.

Nik glared at Lukas then each of the other men in turn. "I want to talk to my brother in private."

"No way," Ewansiha stated. With his arms crossed, he loomed like a bodyguard. A really sexy bodyguard...

Pulling his mind out of the gutter, Lukas added, "Whatever you want to say to him can be said in front of us or not at all."

Nik looked at Xav with a serious expression, and his brother met his gaze. A lot seemed to pass between them. In spite of the tense situation, Lukas experienced a moment where he almost had to fight back a smile at how alike they looked.

"Xav... You don't have to stay here with these guys. You should come home."

Xav swallowed. "Just like that? After everything they said and did?"

"Look, I know it was a bad fight, but you shouldn't have run away. And what the hell do these guys want from you? It's not right." Nik looked extremely uncomfortable.

"Run away? I didn't fucking run away. Is that what they told you? They kicked me out! Told me I wasn't their son anymore...*or* their 'daughter' as Dad put it." He gave a mirthless laugh. "Ran away. I wish! At least then I would've had more than the clothes on my back. And these guys don't want anything from me other than to give me a real home, not a conditional one. Where was all of this brotherly concern when I was being thrown out of the house? You have no idea what I—" Xav stopped abruptly and shook his head.

"I've been trying to find you since I found out. I was so relieved when I saw you were okay. I came straight here. Xav... I know you think you're..." Nik pressed his lips together.

"Gay, Nik. God, you can't even say the fucking word. And I don't *think* it. I *am*. I have been my whole life."

"You don't have to be, though. You just need to try girls, and you'll see—"

Sergio burst out laughing. "I'm sorry, but are you for real? What part of the Stone Age are you from?" He leant forward. "How do you know you're straight, hmm? You just need to try a man..." Sergio winked at him.

Nik recoiled and Lukas was relieved to see Xav grin. "Yeah. That's how I feel about girls. Trust me. When you know, you know." He sobered. "They *hate* who I am, Nik. Hate *me*. And you don't understand me. And that's why I'm staying right here"—he glanced briefly at Lukas and Ewansiha—"as long as I'm welcome."

"You're welcome with us for the rest of your life," Lukas vowed, his heart aching with both pride and pain on Xav's behalf.

"Yes, of course he is." Silvia's melodic voice came from on high.

Every man present snapped his head towards the stairs. Nik's jaw dropped as he saw Silvia stalking down towards them with her finger pointed straight at him. "And *you...*" Even tousled from sleep and wearing a long, faded T-shirt, she was a vision of gorgeousness, but her eyes were snapping with anger.

"You don't deserve him if you can't accept who he is. You don't have to understand it. He's your family." She didn't even stop when she got to the group, but walked right up to Nik and poked his chest—hard. Lukas winced. That had to have hurt with those talon-like nails.

"Grow up and pull your head out of your ass, or you're going to lose your brother forever, you... You..." She burst into tears.

By now, Nik looked terrified. Xav was watching his brother closely as Sergio ushered a weepy Silvia towards the kitchen. Ewansiha stepped forward and brushed shoulders with Lukas, and he felt the boost from that support all the way to his toes.

"Xav?" Lukas prompted when the silence had stretched on. He held an arm out in offering and Xav looked years younger as he moved gratefully into the side-hug.

Nik was taking in their united front with a doubtful expression. "What should I tell Mom and Dad?"

"Honestly? Nothing. Tell me—have they said anything about me to indicate if they care how I'm doing or where I am? I'll bet you didn't even tell them you'd seen me or were coming here today."

Nik dropped his gaze to the floor and shifted his weight.

Lukas felt more than heard the huge sigh Xav gave. "I didn't think so. So why tell them anything at all? I don't care about them any more than they care about me." The way he trembled betrayed that lie.

Ewansiha moved to open the front door and Nik grudgingly took the hint, walking to the threshold before pausing. He drilled Xav with an intense look. "You're sure you're okay here? I'll be done with university in a year then I can definitely get my own place... But if you need me to I could try to afford something sooner..." He trailed off, looking conflicted.

Xav was moving forward from under Lukas' arm before Nik stopped talking. He held out his hand and made a beckoning motion. "Phone." Nik pulled it from his pocket and placed it in Xav's palm. Xav quickly swiped and typed, then handed it back to his brother. "There's my number. Maybe we could text every once in a while?"

Nik seemed to recognise it for the olive branch it was. It was strange and sort of heart-warming to see the two brothers smiling tentatively at each other. It made them look even more alike.

After stepping outside, Nik offered his hand to Ewansiha to shake then to Lukas, who stepped forward to accept the gesture. "No hard feelings. I just want my baby brother to be safe. And happy."

"Us too." Ewansiha said what they were both feeling.

"Um... Can I ask you a favour?" Nik was back to looking uncomfortable again as he looked at King.

Ewansiha frowned. "Sure."

"Could you open the gate so I don't have to climb over the fence again? It was really kind of hard the first time."

Xav burst out laughing, and if it was a bit shaky, that was fine. It had been an emotional scene. Ewansiha was grinning as he walked over to the security panel then typed the code in to open the gate remotely. Nik lifted a hand in farewell then turned away. It was promising that Nik had gone to that much trouble, and Xav must've thought the same thing, because he watched his big brother wistfully as he walked down the drive—probably echoing the way he used to admire him growing up.

After Lukas had closed the door, he leant back against it. "You okay?" he asked Xav.

"Sure," he responded too quickly for it to be anything but automatic. Lukas let it go. Xav would need some time to process things, and hopefully Nik wouldn't let him down.

Lukas' eyes went to Ewansiha, who was watching him sympathetically. Lukas walked straight into his arms and drew strength from that protective embrace. Ewansiha's scent and well-muscled body had a predictable effect on him and he wished they could magically transport themselves home into bed.

He nuzzled into King's neck a little and a hitch in his breathing told Lukas that he wasn't alone in his desire for more than the admittedly nice hug.

"What do you think? Ready to go home?" Ewansiha asked, his voice rumbling his chest against Lukas, who smiled.

"That sounds funny when we're standing in your house. Yeah, after we make sure Silvia's okay." Lukas parted from Ewansiha reluctantly.

"Why wouldn't I be okay?" They turned to see that Silvia's tears were gone, and she looked indignant at the suggestion that she was less than strong.

"Ho-kay, on that note, I think we'll leave you to it, darling." Sergio kissed her cheek then walked towards the front door.

"I think I'll stay here with Silvia tonight," Xav stated, to Lukas' surprise.

"Are you sure?" Ewansiha asked with a puzzled frown.

"Yeah. She shouldn't be alone her first night in a new place. I don't mind. You guys go ahead."

It dawned on Lukas what Xav was trying to do, and he shook his head in wonderment. "Thank you, that's very thoughtful of you." His praise included both the reason he'd given about Silvia, and the unspoken offer to let Lukas and King have a night to themselves.

"Yes, it is," Xav replied cheekily then winked. "Have fun and I'll see you tomorrow."

They gave goodbye hugs to Xav and Silvia, put on their shoes then followed Sergio out. "Don't forget to set the security system after we leave," Ewansiha reminded them.

Both Silvia and Xav rolled their eyes and that was the last impression they were left with as they closed the front door. Ewansiha locked up then they walked to Ewansiha's car, which was in the drive, having been booted from its space in the garage in favour of Silvia's.

"What a day," Lukas sighed as he got into the passenger seat.

Ewansiha climbed in next to him and chuckled. "Yes, and it's not over. Just wait till I get you home."

Lukas smiled as they pulled out of the driveway. "I love it when you call it that."

"I love you."

Lukas whipped his head to look at Ewansiha. Ewansiha was staring straight ahead, but his grip on the wheel betrayed his tension. Thankfully, he could do something about that. "I love you, too, you know."

Subtly relaxing, Ewansiha glanced at him with a little half-smile on his face. "I do now."

Chapter Eighteen

Ewansiha lay on their bed, listening to Lukas finish brushing his teeth. It was nice to think of it as *their* bed instead of Lukas'. He searched for the worry and fear that such a thing usually caused, but there wasn't any, and that was how he knew it was the right thing to do.

He rolled over on his side, tucking his arm under his head. A smile danced along his lips as he imagined what their life would be like in the coming years. They had to help Xav figure out what he wanted in the future. There would be the pitter-patter of little feet running through the house in nine months or so. And who's to say there wouldn't be more children later on when they were ready to take on kids themselves? A baby who looked like Lukas would be beautiful.

Snorting softly, he couldn't believe he was already thinking about more kids, yet they had so much room in their family for more, and Ewansiha didn't think Lukas would be opposed to opening their hearts to others who needed their caring.

A burst of cool air over his ass and the dip of the mattress told him that Lukas had joined him.

Ewansiha sighed as his lover wrapped his arm around his waist, then snuggled close to him. Lukas' hard-on rubbed along Ewansiha's crease, and instead of making him tense, it turned him on even more.

He rarely bottomed, never trusting any man enough to give him that much control over him. Oh, it wasn't that he didn't enjoy it or anything like that. The few times he'd let a guy fuck him, it had been great and he'd come from it, but it wasn't his natural preference. Yet as Lukas rocked against him, he found himself wanting to give Lukas that.

"Can you grab the lube and condom?" he asked, knowing he'd set them on the nightstand next to the bed.

"Sure." He could tell Lukas was smiling just by the inflection in his voice. There was nothing Lukas loved more than having Ewansiha take him. Ewansiha knew that, but he was going to give his lover a surprise tonight.

Rolling over onto his back, Ewansiha took the bottle out of Lukas' hand.

Lukas looked puzzled when Ewansiha paused. "Do you want me to get myself ready?" The gleam in his eyes told Ewansiha that Lukas liked the idea of Ewansiha watching him.

Ewansiha shook his head. "I want you to get me ready, Lukas."

Lukas froze, his hand halfway to his own ass. "What?"

"I want you to make love to me, Lukas. I want this inside me." He wrapped his hand around Lukas' erection, pumping once to draw a moan from Lukas.

"But you don't bottom," Lukas pointed out, even while he pushed on Ewansiha's thighs to get him to spread his legs.

Shrugging, Ewansiha complied with Lukas' demands. He shifted and wiggled until Lukas knelt between his thighs, then he placed one hand behind his knee to pull it up and to the side. Of course, it wasn't the bad knee. He wasn't sure that one would be able to move that way without causing him pain.

"I don't as a general rule, but it's not like I never have. Most of the guys I've been with were just hook-ups at bars and clubs. It wasn't like I knew or trusted them, you know? I've been in three relationships with men before I met you, and I bottomed once or twice for them. I just don't prefer it." He snapped his mouth shut, not sure it was the best thing to talk about former lovers while in bed with his new one.

Lukas chuckled. "I know you've had sex before, King. You're pretty good at it, so you had to have some practice. You decided it was time to give me your ass to keep me from feeling used?"

Shaking his head, he cupped Lukas' cheek with his free hand. "No, babe. I'm not nervous or worried about this like I was with them. Even though I let them top me, I didn't completely enjoy it because it wasn't in my comfort zone. Maybe I knew they weren't the one I was going to spend the rest of my life with. You are, and I want you to know that I love you enough to let you have this."

Lukas surged forward to crush their lips together. Ewansiha slid his hand from Lukas' face to the back of his head, and he let go of his knee to use both hands, holding Lukas there while he feasted on the man's mouth.

He tasted the mint from Lukas' toothpaste, and the underlying flavour of his lover he was addicted to. Lukas braced his hands on either side of Ewansiha's head as they continued to kiss, both moaning as their hard-ons rubbed against each other.

Lukas thrust down, and Ewansiha arched up to meet him. He offered his body up for Lukas to press against, though he wanted the hot length of Lukas' cock inside him. He wanted to feel what it was like to be filled with his lover.

He broke the kiss, panting for a minute to try to catch his breath. When he could finally talk, he said, "I don't want to use condoms anymore."

Lukas jerked in surprise, then met his gaze with a vulnerable expression on his face. "Really? You want to make it exclusive?"

Ewansiha burst out laughing, and hugged Lukas tight to him. "Haven't we been exclusive for the last month or so? I know I haven't dated anyone else, and you've been with me constantly, so I'm pretty sure you're not getting any on the side. Besides, I think me moving in with you would be a clue about how serious I am about our relationship."

Lukas clung to him for a moment. Ewansiha let him, knowing that it was a big moment. Neither one of them had ever had sex without protection, yet Ewansiha knew he wasn't going to be looking for anyone else to share his bed. Lukas was it for him, and he was ready for it all.

"God," Lukas muttered as he pulled away from Ewansiha, then fumbled with the lube bottle. "I'm going to get this all over the place, my hands are shaking so badly."

"Here. Let me." Ewansiha popped open the slick before he squirted some onto Lukas' fingers. "Take it slow because it's really been years since I've bottomed."

"All right." Lukas licked his lips. A hint of worry flared in his eyes, and Ewansiha caressed his shoulder. "Don't worry. You'll be fine, and I'll love it."

Ewansiha closed his eyes and tried to relax as Lukas teased his hole, brushing it with his fingertips before leaving to play with his balls and cock. Soon he found himself surrounded by pleasure on every inch of his groin and ass. Lukas wasn't taking any prisoners as he fisted Ewansiha's length with one of his hands while pressing the tip of a finger inside Ewansiha.

Focusing on Lukas' hand on his cock helped keep Ewansiha from tensing as Lukas slowly invaded his ass with one finger. He stopped to add more lube before he slid two fingers in, while he kept jerking Ewansiha off.

Lust and need swirled around Ewansiha, emotions he'd never felt so much of the other times he'd bottomed. With each stroke of Lukas' fingers, he wanted more. Soon he needed more.

"Lukas, please. I need…" He couldn't find the words to let Lukas know what he wanted.

Luckily for him, Lukas knew exactly what he was longing for. Lukas took one of Ewansiha's hands, then wrapped it around his cock. "Touch yourself while I fuck you. It'll be even more amazing."

The click of the lube bottle signalled Lukas' intent, causing Ewansiha to stiffen slightly. Lukas ran his uncoated hand over Ewansiha's abs and his warm touch soothed his worries. It would be all right because it was Lukas, and his lover would never do anything to hurt him.

He nodded at Lukas' questioning look, then watched as Lukas covered his cock with the slick. As Lukas placed the head of his shaft at Ewansiha's opening, their gazes locked. He thrust forward and

Ewansiha pushed down, meeting Lukas every step of the way.

Once he was as deep as he could get, Lukas froze, and Ewansiha knew it was so he could get used to the almost too-full sensation of Lukas being inside him. The harsh pain mutated into a burning pleasure. He clenched his muscles around Lukas, begging without words for him to move. He wanted Lukas to take him hard and fast, giving him no quarter from desire.

Lukas did that, but he built up to the rough taking, driving Ewansiha to the edge of climax several times, then pulling him back, seeming to want to do his best to ensure that Ewansiha never forgot how it felt to get fucked by Lukas.

Not that he was ever likely to, but still, their first time like this would be burnt into his memory. Ewansiha gripped his erection tight, but simply let Lukas' thrusts push his cock through the tunnel his fingers made. He couldn't focus on doing anything except taking what Lukas did to him.

"Lukas, more. Harder. Please," he pleaded.

There was no warning. One moment he was demanding more. The next he came, spilling cum all over his hand, stomach and even some on his chest. Stars danced before his eyes, he climaxed so hard.

"Fuck, King! You're..." Lukas didn't finish his sentence. He thrust into Ewansiha's trembling body at least three times more before he froze, then flooded Ewansiha's channel with hot cum. "It feels amazing. I never fucked anyone without a rubber. You're so hot and tight... King... I love you."

Ewansiha managed to lift his hand to stroke it over Lukas' sweat-covered chest. "I love you, Lukas. Thank you."

Lukas didn't ask for what, but Ewansiha figured he knew what he meant. Lukas flopped to the side, and Ewansiha moaned as Lukas slid out. Then he wrinkled his nose at the feel of Lukas' cum trickling from his ass. It was hot knowing it was Lukas', but he knew he was going to have to go take a shower before he could sleep.

Pushing up on an elbow, he grinned at Lukas. "You want to go take a shower with me?"

Lukas nodded. "Once I recover enough brain cells to get my body moving, I'd love to."

"We can wait a few minutes."

After lying back, he took Lukas' hand in his, needing his touch to keep him grounded. They entwined their fingers, and Ewansiha smiled. From his very first touch, Lukas had wormed his way into Ewansiha's rather orderly life, and disrupted it. But Ewansiha wouldn't complain because it had got him something he'd never thought he'd ever have.

He'd got a lover who meant the world to him, and a collection of friends who were as close as any family could be. That was worth risking everything in his life for.

About the Author

T.A. Chase

There is beauty in every kind of love, so why not live a life without boundaries? Experiencing everything the world offers fascinates TA and writing about the things that make each of us unique is how she shares those insights. When not writing, TA's watching movies, reading and living life to the fullest.

Devon Rhodes

Devon started reading and writing at an early age and never looked back. At 39 and holding, Devon finally figured out the best way to channel her midlife crisis was to morph from mild-mannered stay-at-home mom to erotic romance writer. She lives in Oregon with her family, who are (mostly) understanding of all the time she spends on her laptop, aka the black hole.

Both authors love to hear from readers. You can find their contact information, website details and author profile page at http://www.totallybound.com.

Totally Bound Publishing

Printed by BoD¨in Norderstedt, Germany